Alexander Cordell's novels have won him wide acclaim as a master storyteller. This tale, the second in a trilogy that began with *The White Cockade,* is at once a lusty adventure story and a moving portrait of an oppressed people at last driven to take a stand.

Witches' Sabbath

ALSO BY ALEXANDER CORDELL

The White Cockade

Witches' Sabbath

Alexander Cordell

THE VIKING PRESS   NEW YORK

For Richard and Christopher Davison of Bargy Castle

First Edition

Copyright © 1970 by Alexander Cordell
All rights reserved
First published in 1970 by The Viking Press, Inc.
625 Madison Avenue, New York, N.Y. 10022
Library of Congress catalog card number: 75–123023

Fic 1. Irish history
Trade 670–77617–3   vlb 670–77618–1
Printed in U.S.A.

1 2 3 4 5   74 73 72 71 70

Contents

Contents / 6

When the hag-fairies dance in the battle's glow
And the swords are a-reap in the tyrant's hand,
When the moon is blood and the traitors know
The stab of the pike and the faltering breath,
When the shout of rebellion flays the land
'Tis a midnight witch and a sabbath of death.
                                        Anonymous

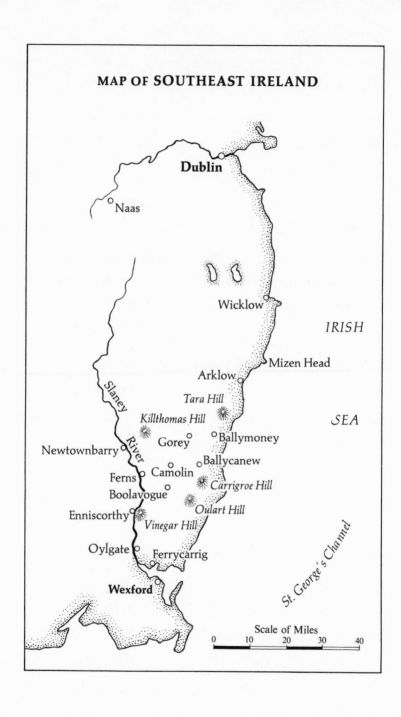

MAP OF **SOUTHEAST IRELAND**

Dublin

Naas

Wicklow

IRISH

Arklow

Mizen Head

Slaney

Tara Hill

Killthomas Hill

SEA

Gorey

Ballymoney

Newtownbarry

River

Ballycanew

Camolin

Ferns

Carrigroe Hill

Boolavogue

Oulart Hill

Enniscorthy

Vinegar Hill

Oylgate

Ferrycarrig

St. George's Channel

Wexford

Scale of Miles

0   10   20   30   40

Rebellion!

I took my big mare fast along the flinted road south to Boolavogue, and the moon was big and ghostly and the hedges like ragged hooligans that ripped and tore at us in the thunder of the hoofs. And Mia raised her great head and neighed at the night sky, I remember, and I could have wept for the joy of having her under me again in this new mission for the sacred soul of Ireland, my country.

"On wi' you, ye big gray thing!" I yelled at her and gripped her mane, crying aloud to her the unintelligible things that horses love, and we went in among the tumps of the fields, flattening over the gates and ditches, taking the brooks in our stride. And above the beating hoofs I seemed to hear the voice of my father urging us on, calling us to duty in the name of the land he loved, and for which he had died.

Insurrection day!

And this was the day for which he had given his life, the dawn of Ireland's rebellion against English rule. For as long as I could remember, my father had been a secret agent for the United Irishmen, the patriots of Belfast and Dublin who had pledged their all to this coming fight for a free and independent land. And now the same pledge was mine. I too had taken the oath to oppose the hated militia and yeomanry regiments, the two-faced Irish soldiery who fought on the side of England, the puppets who sold their birthright to support an English aristocracy and a fawning Irish gentry.

What had happened in France was now happening in Ireland. The bloodbath of the French revolution was glistening red on the clouds over Dublin. From Antrim to Wexford my country was afire.

"Up, up!" I cried. "*Over!*" And Mia leaped high against the stars and sailed over the hedge by the signpost on the road to Naas, and here I reined her in hard and she went up on her hind legs like a bear prancing. For a man was standing in the middle of the lane, a man not much higher than a leprechaun. All dressed up in rebellion green was he, with a cockade hat on his head, a ten-foot pike in one hand, and a bottle of gin in the other.

"*Wheeoh!*" he cried, and he had his pike at Mia's chest in a flash. "Friend or foe is it?" he demanded.

"Friend, old man," I shouted, dismounting.

"Good for you, son." He peered through the moonlight into my face. "You're riding the horse of a giant. Is it boy or man?"

"Seventeen years old," I replied. "And if ye doubt I'm a man you'd best try me."

It is sickening, I think, to have the mind and body of a man but the face of a boy.

His hand went up. "Och, lad—no offense. I was only asking, you see, though it makes little odds. For seventeen or seventy, if you're a loyalist or militia turncoat I'll have ye on the end of this ten-foot pike for toasting."

"Use your eyes," I answered. "I'm wearing the rebel ribbons just the same as you."

"Then why are ye prancing the lanes on that big mare?" he demanded. "If you're a patriot Irish you should be down there marching on the town of Naas under the great Mike Reynolds." His pike trembled under my throat.

"All in good time," I said. "Right now I'm heading for Boolavogue. Is this the right road?"

"It is that, me son, though you'll never see the skies over Boolavogue. For the Armagh Militia under Lord Gosford are coming up it with cannon. And if ye fall among them they'll likely crop your ears and fit ye with a blazing cap like they did me brother." He stared at me, his red-ringed eyes gleaming in his haggard face.

"God rest him," I said. "And God rest you, man, if the militia catch you here."

"Och," said he, tipping the bottle to his lips. "It'll come softer wi' a flask of gin inside me. I've a pike in me hand and a musket in the rocks, and if the Gosford militia crop and singe me it'll be for a good purpose, since I'm not budging from here until Mike Reynolds makes a getaway from Naas."

"Stay if you like, but I'm going."

"Not till you've given me the password."

"For God, for honor, for Ireland," I said.

He lowered the pike. "Right, away wi' ye and God go with you. Which is more than'll happen to this daft loyalist, for he fired at me a hundred paces back and missed." He led me to the roadside undergrowth. A soldier was lying dead there, his eyes open to the stars. The rebel said, "But *I* didn't miss—he didn't know what hit him." Kneeling, he took from the pocket of the dead soldier an envelope. "You reckon this might be important, son? For the trouble is they never taught me to read."

I took the envelope and held it up to the moon and caught my breath as I read:

To Lord Kingsborough, via Lord Gosford, Armagh Militia, Naas, County Kildare

"Is it important?" asked the little rebel, peering over my shoulder.

"It could be life or death," I said, and knelt. With a pencil I rolled back the flap of the envelope, taking the greatest care.

"Are ye opening it, son?"

"I am." Taking out the letter inside, I read:

Wexford now free of insurgents but passage to town still dangerous. Advise you take sea route. Imperative that Wexford be prepared for siege. Report G.O.C. when town is secure. Urgent.

The rebel said, "Och, you're lucky. It's a wonderful thing, mind, to be able to read. Who's that signed by?"

"General Lake," I replied. "The General Officer Commanding."

"General Lake!" the rebel echoed. "The big fella himself?"

I rose. "Aye," I said. "You've found a key that could turn the fate of the country."

"And what will ye do now, then?"

"Make sure that this letter is safely delivered to either Lord Kingsborough or Lord Gosford."

"That's easy. Gosford himself is riding up this road an' he'll be here in less than an hour. Who's delivering it?"

"I am, but I've no time to spend waiting on the roadside."

He prodded me with a finger. "You mean you'd ride into their camp in this rebel rig-out? The Armagh men would burn you alive, son."

"In the uniform of the soldier," I said.

He grunted deep in his chest. "Rather you than me. If they catch you in the uniform of a loyalist they'll treat you as a spy."

"It's the chance I take." I put the letter back into the envelope, rubbed back the gum on the flap, and sealed it. Kneeling, we stripped the dead loyalist of his uniform and I legged myself into his trews and tunic, and they were tight and bandy with me and strangled around the waist and collar. The little rebel laughed. "It's a sorry fate you'll have, lad, wi' your trews splitting up the back when they send ye to kingdom come, but you're a game young cock for all that. What's ye name?"

"John Regan." I folded my rebel uniform under Mia's saddle.

"And where were you off to when I stopped you?"

"To Father John Murphy of Boolavogue—I'm acting on the orders of Lord Edward Fitzgerald."

"Is it a messenger you are, then?"

I went to Mia and swung myself into the saddle. "You could call me that. Are you staying on here?"

But he was not really listening. At the mention of the name Fitzgerald he had crossed himself, and now he was kneeling in the road. Taking a handful of dust, he pressed it against his lips, saying, "To think of it—to think of the honor of it—obeying the commands of a man like Fitzgerald. Ireland will never die, son, while such men live."

"Good-by," I cried, spurring Mia, and I swung down the road toward the Armagh Militia camp.

I looked back once and saw the little rebel still kneeling in the road. He was only five feet high, but it is not the size of the man, my father used to say, but the size of the fight in the man. Alone, he was guarding the road to Naas. And if he shot at a regiment of militia they'd likely crop his ears and hand him the blazing cap of the Hessians, the terrible punishment of the German mercenaries, same as they had given his brother. I looked back again. He was standing now, waving against the stars.

"Ireland will never die while she breeds the likes of you," I said.

Cook-pots were steaming on the side of the road as I walked Mia slowly, my eyes straining to pierce the darkness. And although I knew that I was being watched from the hedges, that they were closing in behind me, there was no sound to betray the presence of loyalist militia. For this was a regiment feared by the peasantry; these Irish volunteer soldiers fought against their brothers in support of the English Crown. Units such as this now marching on Naas to engage the patriot Irishman Mike Reynolds were the men who were laying waste to my country, hanging men and even women without trial on the orders of a corrupt Irish Parliament which was the tool of England. I hated them, but I also feared them. For years soldiers such as these had tormented my people and bled them white, turning them into vassals of the aristocracy. Now, in the year 1798, the peasants were rising against their tyranny. On all sides rebel regiments were being formed to drive these parasites from the land. And men like Lord Edward Fitzgerald and Wolfe Tone were leading us; men like Neilson and Lawless, Bagenal Harvey and Matthew Keugh, were becoming the heroes of my generation.

I reined in now, my body stiffening to the chink of arms. Moonlight flashed on a scabbard; faintly I heard muffled breathing. And, of a sudden, they rose about me along the hedgerows and barred the road before me. Hands reached up for me, dragging me down. I saw their faces in that faint light, square, strong, and brutal. The man who spoke was short and broad, and his voice was guttural.

"What your name?"

I knew him instantly for a German mercenary.

"John Regan," I said.

"What regiment?"

I thought quickly. "North Cork Militia," I answered, "attached to headquarters in Dublin. I am a messenger."

They crowded about me; lanterns were lit and thrust into my face. One laughed softly and gabbled something in a foreign tongue.

I said sharply, "Take me to Lord Gosford."

"You got a very good horse here, soldier." He seized Mia's rein and walked her in a circle, grunting approval. "We give you five shilling for the horse, messenger."

I said evenly, "Take me to Lord Gosford or one of the Irish militia, for I have a message from Dublin and I am not speaking to Germans."

The man paused, dropped the rein, and approached me. "You got a cheeky tongue, boy. You talk to Hompesch regiment, do you know?"

"And it is better I talk to Irish."

I despised even the name of this German regiment; they had tortured and brutalized my countrymen.

The man turned away, muttering, "One day you pray to us, eh? You cross us in fighting one day and we will take you. Then you will not know Irish from German."

"Perhaps," I replied. "Now take me to Lord Gosford, or his adjutant will have you flogged."

His dark eyes shifted in his ravaged face and he spat at my feet. "Today you win, then, but the Hessians will remember your face, eh? Come."

I followed him down the moonlit road. The Armagh Militia were here with their little square cannon ready for the attack on Naas, which was held by the rebels. Feet up in the ditches they lay, their faces betraying their disgust at the German who was leading me; for although they were allies of the Hompesch, they also hated and feared them. Outside a tent in a little clearing I waited, and almost instantly the German reappeared with an Armagh captain. Clicking my heels, I saluted. My tongue was dry in my mouth.

"Messenger from Dublin, sir," I said. "I have a letter for Lord Gosford or Lord Kingsborough."

The captain, young and handsome, was possessed of a quiet charm. Smiling, he asked, "What regiment, soldier?"

"North Cork, sir."

I could have bitten off my tongue. Lord Kingsborough, I suddenly remembered, was colonel of the North Cork Militia. The lie, now told, would have to be perpetuated.

"Give me the message," said the adjutant captain.

I said, "With respect, sir, I am to hand the letter either to Lord Kingsborough or Lord Gosford—no other."

"Do not be ridiculous. Hand it over. It will be safe with me."

I stood rigidly at attention. We stared at each other and he began to smile slowly, rubbing his chin. "Well done," he said. "The North Cork are improving. Come this way."

The German soldier glowered at me as I followed the captain to a wayside tent. Lord Kingsborough was sitting at a map table within the tent. I recognized him immediately, having seen him five months ago at Rudd's Inn down in Enniscorthy, when on the last mission with my father. Kingsborough, thank heaven, had not seen me. The captain said, "A messenger from Dublin, sir."

"From General Lake, sir," I said.

Lord Kingsborough raised his tired face to mine. "The man gives me no peace," he said. "What does he want of me now?" Reaching out, he took the offered letter and ripped open the envelope. His eyes were expressionless as he read slowly. Tossing the letter down on the table, he rose and began to pace the room.

Unaccountably, I knew no fear. Now that I was totally committed, fear had gone. My life was completely in this man's hands. On the faintest suspicion he could have me hanged, or worse—handed over to the Hompesch dragoons for the torture of the pitch cap. Next to the British General Lake, this Lord Kingsborough was one of the most despised but important men in the country. Standing there before him, I reflected that he would make an excellent hostage if ever the rebel army needed to bargain.

Suddenly he said, as if to himself, "You are a long way south, soldier."

"Yes, sir."

"What is your regiment?"

I flashed a glance at the watching adjutant. "North Cork, sir."

"Indeed? My own regiment." He peered at my tunic, his faded eyes coming alive in his face. "Attached to General Headquarters?"

"In Dublin, sir."

His eyes moved over me and he sat back in his chair, smiling faintly. "Your name?"

"John Regan, sir." I could have lied, but I had

already given my name to the German soldiers. Lies are awkward, blundering betrayers; once they are told they have to be remembered, and I am not good at lying.

Kingsborough said, "Not only the face but the name is strangely familiar. Have you relatives serving under me?"

"No, sir."

He nodded and I fought for outward calm. Inside me a nagging fear was growing. True, he had not seen me when we shared the roof of Rudd's Inn five months back, but without a doubt my father would have been well known to him. To my relief, he shrugged, saying, "I pride myself that I never forget a face. You have served me well, Regan—I shall not forget yours. Report back to your unit." He dismissed me with a cursory wave of the hand.

"This way," said the captain.

The Hessians watched me as I rode Mia past them along the road to the north, and the one who stopped me coming in wandered beside my stirrup.

"You remember me, soldier?"

"I do."

He raised his lantern high. In the other hand he held a short, thick flogging whip. "One day we meet, soldier—just you and me, eh?"

"I'll look forward to that," I said.

"And with this whip I shall cut you in two."

It was disgusting to have to breathe the same air he did. Spurring Mia away, I took her at a gallop out of the camp. The air was sweet and clean, I remember, and the stars were sprinkled all over the dark sky. I rode faster still, taking the open country and turning south for Enniscorthy the moment I thought it safe.

And as we thundered down the ragged lanes I saw the road before me snaking like a silver ribbon across the hills. I was now bent on a mission of greater importance than that Lord Fitzgerald had commanded me. He had merely ordered me to report to Father John Murphy of Boolavogue, to support a parish priest and raise a standard of insurrection. Now I was carrying a secret that could affect every man, woman, and child in the country.

Clash of Arms

Privately speaking—since there are two sides to every man—there was a need in me for the bright eyes of a girl called Kathleen who lived down Enniscorthy way.

It's a queer thing being seventeen years old, for when you're younger the women seem all string bean and carroty or as fat as plum pudding with crabapple knees. But when you're turned seventeen it's a different shape they do put on themselves: coming all willowy and peaches-and-cream, with hair flowing to their waists—just like this Kathleen Lehane I mentioned, who lived with her father at Rudd's Inn. And although I was partial to old Joe Lehane because he was a United Irishman, I was also becoming keen about his offspring, and she about me. So I took Mia even faster across the country toward Enniscorthy, and when the light of dawn was flowing over the hills I rode her into the reeds of a little river and we put ourselves to bed there and dreamed.

Mia, I reckon, dreamed of oats, as horses likely do, and I suppose I should have dreamed of Father John Murphy, to whom I was reporting on the orders of Lord Fitzgerald. Instead, I dreamed of someone a foot shorter and ten stones lighter, one dressed in pink and with black hair about her shoulders, for the tap maids come pretty in Joe Lehane's place down in Enniscorthy.

Och, dear me.

I reached Ferns late that afternoon and was directed on to Boolavogue, which was in the parish of Father John, and the peasants were sullen with me because of my loyalist uniform. There was a smell of burning and rebellion in the air. And when I rode into Boolavogue I saw flames shafting the sky and smoke billowing over the land, and more than once I went flat under the hedges to the explosions of muskets.

Reining Mia through the trees, I took her slowly, getting the size of things, and on the edge of a wood

I halted her, staring into the road. Here several houses and a little Catholic chapel were burning, and the hated loyalists were rushing around the flames shrieking while the villagers let into them with pitchforks and pikes. The commotion they were making was enough to raise a churchyard.

In the shelter of the trees I changed out of the loyalist uniform and back into my rebel green.

I did not know, as I did this, that I had come to the place that was the very beginning of the Wexford rebellion.

I saw a priest standing alone, and in his hands he held a crucifix, and around him knelt his parishioners, watching their chapel burn.

"Is it Father John Murphy, sir?" I asked, standing to attention before him.

"It is," said he, not sparing me a glance. His eyes were on the flames engulfing his chapel, and I saw in his face the stamp of greatness. Big was he, with a good square jaw on him and the shadows deep in his brow. And the blaze of the fire colored him in red.

Drawing near him, I said, "Father John. Lord Edward Fitzgerald himself ordered me to report to you, and I have important news concerning Lord Kingsborough—I was standing before him yesterday. May I speak with you?"

His face turned slowly to mine; he was not really

listening. "Important news, is it? Is anything more important in the world than the state of things here?" His voice rose above the crackle of the flames and the noise of the fighting. "Does a priest stand by idly while his parishioners are flogged and his chapel burned?"

I did not reply. It was not the time to tell of Kingsborough. For the peasants were flocking about the great man now, their hands red with the blood of the yeomanry. They thrust their hands mutely before him, as if in evidence of their crime. The priest cried then, "As He whipped them out of the temple, the men of greed, so we take vengeance on the burning of His house. There is no wickedness in the spilling of blood like this!"

"Aye, aye!" They linked hands; they cried aloud in relief.

"And I killed two—can ye hear me, Father John?" shouted a man.

"I hear all who are prepared to fight for Ireland!"

"But the main party are away, Father!" cried another. "Within the hour Lieutenant Bookey and another regiment of yeomen will be arrivin'!"

"Then prepare to receive them—away and find arms, man!" Father John rose to his great height. "Fight, fight! By holy God, if Bookey arrives he'll put his fingers in a nest of asps. *Och*, if he comes we

will play him a devil's tune for every decent creature on the land from Dublin to Wexford!" He strode
among them, a giant in strength and purpose, and
the greatness in him seemed to lift them from their
despair. And I saw in him a man of vision, born in
this hour of Ireland's destiny. He swung to me.

"You, son, you!"

"Aye, Father!"

"Away on that horse and warn the people. Raise
the alarm between Camolin and Oulart, pull them
from their beds between Ferns and Enniscorthy. Tell
them that the church is with them, that God has
raised the banner of freedom! *Away!*"

In the light of the flames I left him. And thus will
I always remember him: as the man who stood in
fire, watching his house and chapel burning, and
with the half-starved wretches of his parish scurry-
ing about him or kneeling in the road making up
weapons. Pike-heads were appearing from nowhere,
and pope's heads—the great brush brooms—being
stripped for sharpening. At last released from their
bondage of fear, the peasants were shouting with
joy. But even as I leaped onto Mia's back and spurred
her from the blazing chapel, a great shout arose
among the milling peasants: "The yeomanry, the yeomanry!"

I swung Mia back, reining her up, and the ragged

defenders rose about Father John, their ill-fashioned pikes held before them.

"Bookey is coming! Bookey is coming!" It was the old cry of terror, and I scrambled Mia in behind the mob and saw, on the road that led to Gorey, the flash of steel and heard the shouted *hurrahs* as the sabers came out.

"The cavalry!"

"Aye!" roared Father John. "The cavalry, and you will stand. Forward with the pikes, *forward!*"

Down the road came the horsemen, three abreast, their sabers waving. But within a hundred yards of the burning chapel, the front horses reared up at an ambush of rolling logs. Skidding, they fell, and the on-ward rush of those behind carried them into the ambush as well. The horses pranced in a melee of fallen yeomen, and from the trees the peasants darted with leveled pikes. Shouting every Irish war cry from Skibbereen to Ballycastle, they drove the pike-heads home, slashing at the reins to bring the horses down, freed at last from the paralyzing fear that for years had branded them and bought them slavery. Spurring Mia, I took her along the edge of the battle, slashing and piercing with my rapier, aiming always for the shoulder. And the yeomen fell like wheat before the peasants. Writhing under the stabbing pikes, scrambling away into the woods, they were defeated and scattered in a battle of five minutes. The moment before I left the scene I saw Lieutenant Bookey, dead beneath his dying horse, his breast transfixed by a pike.

"Away!" shouted Father John, running up. "Away and rouse them, and bring them here—d'ye know Killthomas Hill, son?"

"I can find it, Father!"

"And Oulart?"

"That I do!"

"Split the men between the two. Tell them to camp on the high ground. You understand?"

"Aye!"

"But all within a mile send here—women, too, remember—and tell them to bring arms!" In the dying flames the peasants crowded about us in fear.

There was a sudden silence, broken only by the groans of the wounded and the clatter of Mia's hoofs, and Father John shouted, "Well, do ye hesitate now the deed is done?"

In abject terror, as realization began to strike them, the peasants of Boolavogue stared up at him, and he raised his fist and cried into their faces, "Do not stare at me, for the die is cast. You have taken arms against the Crown. You are already committed, mark me! It is nothing but fight now, because there is naught to lose. Are you with me?"

As if released, they leaped toward him, crying his name.

" 'Tis fight and die, for nothin' remains. If there's a hundred patriot Irish here tonight there'll be a hundred nooses made by morning, but I tell ye this, people—if die ye do, you die in the name of God, for it's a stink in the noses of decent Irish to live the lives of cowards and felons. Are ye on?"

As the clamor grew, as they crowded about him to shake his hands and cry his name, I spurred Mia away.

I remember there was blood on my hands, yeomen's blood, as I made my way into a full May moon and galloped like a madman for Ferns and Enniscorthy.

The die, as Father John Murphy had said, was surely cast. The rebellion had begun.

The Approaching Storm

For ages rapine ruled the plains,
And slaughter raised his red right hand;
And virgins shrieked and roof-trees blazed,
And desolation swept the land.

Anonymous

The moon was still high as I galloped Mia through Camolin and Ferns, and at each place I lit a bonfire in the street and the people gathered around me, shouting for news, with their night clothes scragged about them and their gaunt faces red in the light of the fire.

"Father John of Boolavogue says to take to arms—

to find high ground on Oulart and await him there!"

"The rebellion! The rebellion!" They shouted, they cheered, they danced in the street.

"Women, too—everybody who can carry arms— away to Oulart Hill and Killthomas!"

"Oulart Hill! Oulart Hill!" The cry was taken up. Doors were coming open and men and women were tumbling out, crying the beloved name, "Father Murphy! 'Tis Father John himself biddin' us!"

They knelt and made the sign of the cross; they prayed.

"Is it a trap? Who's the lad?"

"A messenger from Father Murphy! And the yeomanry's been beaten at Boolavogue!"

"D'ye hear that, Reilly? The standard's been raised in Boolavogue!"

"Bookey's been killed and the yeomen scattered!"

"Who says this?"

"The lad here!"

Surrounded by scores of them, I held up my hand, crying, "It's freedom or the rope now! Away wi' you all—to Oulart Hill and Killthomas!"

Pitchforks were coming out; men and women were girding on rusted swords. Pike handles were fetched and distributed, and people kneeled on the cobbles, striking on the iron heads. Torches were lighted. A few minutes earlier Ferns and Camolin were asleep; now they were alive with insurgents. The peasants clutched Mia's saddle, turning with her as she pranced; they caught my hands, kissing them. And as I galloped down the road to Enniscorthy I saw over my shoulder the thin lines of torches from Ferns and Camolin massing into a gigantic bonfire of rebellion that streamed east for Oulart Hill and Killthomas in fiery lanes.

On, on to Enniscorthy now, lying flat over Mia for fear of a musket ambush, ready to leap roadblocks that were never encountered. For the militia and yeomen were under their beds, it was said, when news of the victory at Boolavogue reached them, but this I will never believe.

Lying under their beds in trembling fear, is it?

Och, indeed: we knew better later.

Before reaching Enniscorthy I struck across the fields and roused the people in the hamlets. In the early flushes of a watery dawn, they streamed from their beds as they had done at Ferns and Camolin, eager for battle. From farm to farm I rode and cabin to cabin, raising the neighborhoods to the revolution. Other messengers from Boolavogue were at work, too, for I saw them as I came up to Enniscorthy. And by morning the roads and lanes were so packed with rebels that I had to take to the fields. I rode until Mia was exhausted, and then, when the task was done, I crossed the Slaney and trotted into Rudd's Inn.

"John Regan!"

It was Kathleen Lehane, and pretty enough for eating was she, leaning out of the window with her long black hair either side of her face and her cheeks glowing pink. Then she slammed the window and I heard her belting up to her father as to how John Regan was in the yard and up ye get this minute and see to his nag while I cook breakfast. And I was getting off Mia and leading her to the stable for oats when she comes into the yard, does this Kathleen, with her hands behind her back in a civil sort of stroll, and ducks alive, what brings ye here at this time o' the mornin'?

"It's the rebellion," I said, for the last thing I wanted was to appear too keen on seeing her.

"Didn't ye come to see us, then—me and me pa?"

"Not necessarily," said I. "Just happened I was this side of the Slaney."

With this she went cool on me and stomped her feet around the yard and pouted. Her lips were scarlet and beautiful in the pink sheen of her skin, and I'd seen nothing like her in all me travels, but this was the last thing I was telling her for it's daft to let them in on too much.

"Is it well wi' ye?" she asked at length.

"As well as can be expected," said I, "considering the state of the country. Don't ye realize that Father

Murphy has raised the first standard at Boolavogue
an' that the land is in open revolution?"

"Didn't ye miss me, then, during your travels up
in Dublin with Lord Fitzgerald?" she asked, peeved.

"Och, woman, I had no time to give ye a thought."

Mia, I recall, gave us a queer kind of glance, and I
was just boxing and bedding her when Kathleen's
father came into the yard.

This man, insignificant in appearance and bald,
was my father's friend. As proprietor of Rudd's Inn,
he entertained friend and foe alike, yet for as long
as I could remember he had been a secret agent
for the United Irishmen of Belfast and Dublin. The
great and the famous stayed with Joe Lehane when
they visited Enniscorthy—men like Lord Kingsborough, whom I had seen here on my last visit with
my father—and it was said in secret circles that more
intelligence was handed to the patriot army by Joe
Lehane than by any other ten agents of the rebellion.

"Can ye bide a minute, Joe?" I whispered.

He nodded and entered the stable, pulling the door
behind him.

"Have you heard the rebellion's on?" I asked.

"I have," said he, and there was a great and awful
sadness in him. "And I tell ye this, youngster—Ireland's not ready to rise."

"Would ye have her sink under the whip, then?"

I asked. "How long d'you think decent men like Father Murphy can stand the sight of the burnings and floggings? If we don't rise now, man, we'll never rise at all."

"You're young, and you're hot," said little Joe, "but you're wrong!"

I raised my voice. "Father John Murphy was sent by God!"

"And he'll meet his God sooner because of it." Joe made a fist of his hand. "I tell ye this, John— and if your father was alive today he'd be in agreement with me—they're begging us to rise, they want us to revolt too soon. And they'll pick off this rebellion like a boy stamping out bonfires."

I waved him down. "*Och*, be sensible, Joe, it is now or never. When we get into the swing of it Wolfe Tone will land with a French fleet in support, and we'll drive the English back to Bristol."

"In your dreams," said Joe, mournfully. "Have ye heard Lord Fitzgerald's been taken?"

"What?" I stared at him. "It can't be—I was with him four days back."

"Then you're two days late. They took him at Thomas Street, Dublin, and he fought for it and wounded one of them sore. But they shot him in the shoulder, and now the leader's lying in Newgate gaol an' his life is despaired of."

I sat down on a saddle. Sweat sprang to my face. Only four days ago the leader of the rebellion had given me my orders to report to Father John; now he was wounded and captured.

Joe groaned, his hand to his head. "There's a sad row to hoe yet, son, but it is the beginning of the end."

"But you'll still fight for it?" I asked.

"I was fighting for Ireland, son, before you were born."

"And would a hostage be of any use to you?"

"If we lose the early rounds there'd be nothing better than a hostage." He grinned, filling his clay pipe. "And who might you have in mind—the King of England?"

"Lord Kingsborough of the North Cork."

Joe laughed. "You're the son o' your father when it comes to aiming high."

"Come closer," I said.

I told him of the meeting with the little rebel outside Naas, and of the letter we took from the dead North Cork soldier, and how I delivered it to Lord Kingsborough. I told him that I thought Kingsborough would sail for Wexford within a few days, after the battle of Naas.

"He was outside Naas with the Armagh Militia, you say?" asked Joe.

"He was—waiting to attack Mike Reynolds, who was marching on the town—and he was in the company of the murderous Hessians."

"Then he'll deserve all he gets," said Joe reflectively, and added, "He'll likely sail from Mizen Head, and I know that coast like the back of my hand. I've a wee ketch laid up there and it seems she'll come in handy. Can you think of the joy of it—steering Kingsborough himself up the hill to the gaol in Wexford town?"

"I'd give an arm to see that," I replied.

Joe wandered about, excited. "I'll pass this on to Caine Adams—he could make use of Kingsborough if we fall on hard times. Have ye mentioned this to a living soul, John?"

"I was all set to tell Father Murphy, but he had his hands full with the parishioners of Boolavogue."

"Keep it that way—not a single word. Where are ye off to now, then?"

"For some of Kathleen's rice pudding," I said. "She turns out the finest rice pudding this side of Dublin. Will you feed and bed me, Joe, for the few hours until I ride to Father John for the squabble on Oulart Hill?"

"And welcome," said Joe. "There's nothing like a double helping of Kathleen's pudding for keeping out the bullets."

Death of a Rebel

The church bells were ringing for early mass when I awoke, with Kathleen bursting into the bedroom without the grace of a knock, and she cried, "We just heard some terrible news!"

The shock of her flushed me out like a ferreted rabbit, but I was back under the clothes next instant, for all I was wearing was my brief cotton trews.

"What's up, woman?" I said.

"Killthomas Hill—the rebels have been routed on Killthomas!"

In came Joe Lehane then, shocked white like a ghost and shaking. "It's true, man. Two hundred fifty yeomen have beaten ten times that number of rebels up on Killthomas height. Nigh two hundred rebels have been killed and the rest runnin' for their lives!"

I was out of that bed then, cotton trews or not, and Kathleen cried, "And the yeomen are burning the cabins and shooting innocent people!"

"And priests have died wi' the rebels, too," whispered Joe, crossing himself. "Catholic priests, and two of them I knew . . ."

I froze, praying for Father John.

"Is there news of a battle at Oulart?"

"Aye, no, but the North Cork Militia under Colonel Foote are advancing on Oulart this minute, an' it's said he'll cut Father John and his rebels to bits, like at Killthomas."

Kathleen put her hands over her face. "Burning the cabins and killing the people. I canna stand it!"

"Even women and children," added Joe, clenching his fists in anguish.

"I'll believe that when I see it," I said, flapping into my shirt and leggings. "The yeomen may be mad dogs on men, but I've yet to see them at women and kids." I flared up at Kathleen then. "Why did ye let me sleep so late, woman?"

"It saved your life," said she, "for sure you'd otherwise have been fighting with them on Killthomas."

"Are you away now, then?" asked Joe, following me down the stairs.

"I am that. D'you expect me to be lying in bed with Father John up on Oulart Hill!" I rushed past him to the stable where Mia was still dozing as if tomorrow would do, and I reckon she was still at it until I got the spurs into her and wheeled in the yard. Kathleen came out, her hair flying, and caught my hand and put it against her face.

"You'll come back, John? Swear ye'll return?"

"If I have a hand in it, girl. And the next time call me when you're told to or there'll be the devil to pay rent to!" I gave her a grin and a wink, and I was away over the cobbles and along the road to Oulart Hill.

Only the tolling of the bells of Enniscorthy told me that it was Whitsunday. Dimly tolled those bells, as if over the funeral pyre that once was my country.

I took across country, leaping the ditches, clearing the hedges in bounds. For they told me the roads were packed with loyalist militia, though there was no sign yet of regular English troops. And now, on high ground, I saw a party of Foote's North Cork soldiers marching for distant Oulart, and fearsome they looked in their fine array of uniforms and arms. They were mostly on foot, but a few cavalry were leading and the fierce sun of morning flashed on their cannon. I reckoned that with Mia fresh and strong I would cut them off and reach Oulart first, to give news of the coming attack. I was about to spur away when I heard a voice.

"Water!"

Clear as the tolling bells of Enniscorthy, I heard that voice, and I stood up in the stirrups, looking around, but nothing moved in the thick ferns.

"*Water!*"

I heard the voice again and saw with it a wave of the heather, and I slipped off Mia and ran to the place, parted the green, and found a man.

He was young, about my own age. Blood was on his face and his green rebel doublet was stained heavy with the stuff. His hair, I remember, was the color of ripe corn, and there was upon his face no beard or stubble. And then, kneeling closer, I saw that he was just a youngster—twelve years old, no more.

"What ails ye, boy?" I asked him, and raised his head.

He said, "Are ye with me, sir, or agin me?"

"I'm a rebel, same as you. What are you doing up here above Enniscorthy?"

He said, his voice firm now, "I was up on Kill-thomas Hill and fought with Father Patrick and Father Sweeney, but both are dead."

"And where d'you live?" I raised him higher. "What's your name?"

"Enniscorthy," he replied, "and me name's Jeff Hays."

"But you nigh passed through Enniscorthy in comin' up here, son!"

"That I did—last night, after the battle. Listen, sir, can ye hear the sound of the bells for mass?"

I nodded.

He smiled, his eyes filled with tears. "Aye, it's a sweet sound indeed. Water, please, for the love of God."

I ran and got my pannikin and filled it with water from a trickling stream and seeped it between his lips and washed his face with a cloth. He laid back his bright hair in the heather and sighed, then, like a man sighs when the nails go through his hands.

"But why didn't you go home in Enniscorthy?" I whispered.

"Because the militia were after me, and I would lead them to my mother."

I clenched my hands.

"Can ye hear the sound of the bells, sir?" he asked again.

"That I can."

"And will you do a thing for me, when you get back to Enniscorthy?"

"I will that." I gripped his hands.

"Will you go to see my mother and tell her I was with Father Patrick and Father Sweeney? Will ye tell her that I went with them to keep the country decent, like Father Patrick said?" He pulled from his neck a little silver locket and chain. "And will ye hand this to me mother? It's a hair lock of me father, but it rightly belongs to her. He's fighting with Father Murphy, ye see, and his name and address are inside."

"I will see that she gets it," I replied, taking the locket.

"That's grand, then," said he. "But isn't it a pity the bells have stopped their tolling for mass?"

But they had not stopped tolling; they rang louder and louder, as if in appeal to the souls of men. I bowed my head for the rebel aged twelve.

"Good-by, man," I said in the scald of tears.

They sniped at me when I reached the foot of Oulart Hill, and then did it again and the ball cut a groove in a tree beside me and whined away on the wind. I dismounted in case Mia should collect the next one, and pulled out a white cloth and waved it above my head. At this a sentry rose from behind a distant rock. All done up and fine was he, with a woman's wig on his pate and a wand of heather in his musket and his legs rigged up in a set of bright red woman's

pantaloons. Blue was his tunic, with brass buttons
on his waistcoat and a cutlass dangling from his
belt like a pirate of the Spanish Main. Raising his
musket, he threatened me, drunk as a coot.

"Put that thing down and let me by to Father John
Murphy, and quick," I said.

"Does ye life depend on it then, sir?" he asked.

"Your life," I replied, "for the North Cork are
comin' to collect rebels' ears."

Very partial to rebels' ears were the North Cork,
God forgive them.

"You can't get to Father John quick enough," said
he, at attention. "Pass, friend, all is well."

And I walked through the lines just like that, and
I could have been the King of England.

This was the trouble with the Irish rebellion. You
learn how to make war with a musket in your hands
from men who know of war, but the Irish rebels were
learning from priests who didn't know a pike from
a gun or a poniard from a pulpit. It was terrifying
to think that two hundred fifty Irish militia could
rout two thousand five hundred rebels up on Killthomas Hill.

I found Father John at prayer on the highest point
of Oulart, with several thousand rebels kneeling
about him. I knelt also, and he cried, " 'Woe to him
that buildeth a town with blood, and stablisheth a

city by iniquity! For lo, I raise up the Chaldeans, that bitter and hasty nation, which shall march through the breadth of the land to possess the dwelling places that are not theirs. They are terrible and dreadful: their judgment and their dignity shall proceed of themselves.' "

A great murmur grew among the kneeling men, and the earth trembled beneath me to that sound, such were their numbers. I looked above my clasped hands and saw Father John with his arms flung up to the sky, his fists shaking in fury as he cried, " 'Shall they not rise up suddenly that shall bite thee? And awake that shall vex thee. . . . Because thou hast spoiled many nations, all the remnants of the people shall spoil thee; because of men's blood, and for the violence of the land, of the city, and of all that dwell therein'!"

And again there came from that kneeling multitude a low sighing, as of assent, and it grew louder, as if in anger. Then, of a sudden, the kneeling multitude rose about me, and from their throats came a bass and terrible roar that rose to the heavens. The sound filled me with terror. It held an animal fury that was a stain on the souls of men. And it transformed this Sunday, the day of church bells and goodness, into an evil and unearthly day, a day of bloodshed and inhumanity. A witches' sabbath.

Howling, they raised their arms like a forest, and Father Murphy, perched against the sky on a high mound, raised up a great crucifix, and then all was silent. The morning blazed with sun, and from a sky of blue a great light flashed on the crucifix of the Lord our God, until Father John lowered it and held it against him. The army knelt.

"Amen!"

The word resounded over Oulart Hill like a dark wind, and I gripped my hands and lowered my face from the blinding brilliance of the sun.

"Amen," they said. "Amen!"

Leaping to my feet, I raced up the hill through the packed ranks of the kneeling rebels, pushing them from my path and shouting, "Father John, Father John! The North Cork are coming!"

Charge on Oulart Hill

"The North Cork, the North Cork!"

The rebels recoiled in a panic as the word went round.

"The North Cork are comin'!"

They milled about on Oulart Hill, kneeling to prime their rusted muskets and keen the blades of their pikes on stones. Here and there ancient muskets exploded and men fell in groans as useless flintlocks blew up in their hands. I myself saw one man fall, his breast transfixed by the ramrod of his own muzzle-loader, for as he rammed the powder the rod had sparked. Hunting horns were blowing; platoon lead-

ers were whistling shrilly with their fingers, fighting
to get some semblance of order. And I saw, on the
road below the hill, the North Cork Militia coming
with the calm that flows from trained soldiery. With
their little band of cavalry jogging at their head they
came, disdainful of the shouting, half-starved rabble
they had come to cut to pieces.

The North Cork Militia numbered little more than
a hundred. Little more than a hundred soldiers, remember, and we were four thousand!

Slapping Mia in the belly, I dropped behind a
boulder, and she went flat beside me like a horse
already dead, for in this my father had trained her.
And through a groove of the boulder, I saw the North
Cork infantry deploying calmly around the base of
the hill, now squirming flat toward us, their bunch-
ing hips and punching elbows cutting through the
undergrowth like oncoming snakes. Now they were
up and running silently, and before we had time to
raise a musket they were flat on the rocks again.
Relentlessly they came, undaunted by the knowledge
that they were outnumbered by forty to one. But
then Father John's voice rang out loud and clear:

"Hold your fire, men, hold your fire!"

Silence. The morning sang in bird song and heat.
I heard nothing but the faint rustling of the heather
and the chinking of harness as the North Cork, with

a section of the German Hompesch dragoons, moved their cavalry in on the road from Enniscorthy.

Close behind the boulder, I primed my pistol and shoved it into my belt, then drew the rapier, eyes narrowed to the fierce sunlight, watching the enemy advance in quick flushes of the heather. And at that moment a woman began to sing in a deep contralto, her voice sweet and clear, and I heard the words of the old Irish ballad:

> The sodgers ir comin'! Rin fast, rin fast; wi' guns and wi' bayonets! Rin fast, rin fast! They're lukin' for guns, an' they're lukin' for pikes! They'll show ye no mercy, the bloodthirsty tykes!

And at the end of that song the morning screamed into life. The heather parted and the North Cork stood up, pouring a sudden volley of fire into the hillside, and all about me rebels flung up their hands and toppled down. Down into the heather went the North Cork, and nothing moved on that hill save the writhing figures of the rebels who had been shot down. Up again now, these North Cork, like puppets on a string, and tongues of flame spurted death from their reprimed muskets, and more rebels fell, some rolling head over heels down through the ranks of the oncoming militia.

"Fire when they stand, ye fools!" yelled Father

John close behind me, and a loud, ragged cheer came from the rebels as they heard the beloved voice. "Fire when they stand, men—ready now!"

Again and again the North Cork rose from behind the boulders, each time coming closer to the summit of the hill, and now the staccato fire of the rebels met them, but few had muskets and fewer still knew how to use them. And suddenly, as if transported toward us by some evil magic, the militia rose for the last time, fired, and charged. Led by their gallant young officers, urged on by the harsh commands of their sergeants, they charged up the last slopes with fixed bayonets. All about me the rebels broke and ran, and instantly the soldiers were among them with the bayonets, thrusting, stabbing. From behind the boulder I took careful aim and fired, and a North Cork clutched at his leg and fell, tumbling down the slope. I was priming the pistol when the next was upon me—an officer, this one, and I saw his face clearly as he slashed down at me with his saber. It was the big Hompesch dragoon who had threatened me at Kingsborough's headquarters. His blade swished the air an inch above my head as I went flat and rolled into the undergrowth, and he was upon me instantly, cutting and stabbing as I parried and fought him off. North Cork and Germans were leaping past us as I scrambled up and faced him square, and there seemed only the two of us in the world then, despite the clatter and roar of the battle.

"You remember me, eh? North Cork, you say?" He lunged and I parried him. "Rebel swine, I kill you for sure now!" And he bore me backward in a flash of steel. The charge of the militia surged past us; in a pit ringed with stones we faced each other, blades out, circling, and I saw his eyes shining at the prospect of the fight. Cannonades from the little trundle cannons of the North Cork were reverberating over the hill, and I heard the rebel women screaming as the enemy got among them. But I also sensed something else in the fighting around me, a stiffening of the rebel will, a loss of fear, the beginning of a counterattack. The sheer numbers of our forces were beginning to tell. And above the thunder of the battle came Father John's deep voice:

"Rally, lads, rally! Conquer or perish, remember. Into them, into them, in the name of God!"

The German came again, shouting a hoarse war cry, darting and thrusting under my guard, but I backed away still, letting him tire himself. He was no longer young and already he was breathing heavily, his face inflamed with the poteen they brewed in the little wayside stills. And as his anger increased so did his lumbering charges, and I knew I would have to finish him quickly. Only once before had I killed a man, and the memory of it stayed with me in my dreams, but I knew I would have to kill this one. He had recognized me. He had seen me first in North Cork uniform, now in rebel green. And if he lived, even wounded, he would report what he knew to Kingsborough's headquarters.

Now the German came again, his rapier a whir of light in the instant before he set himself for the thrust. I side-stepped and the blade flashed an inch clear of my side. Off balance, the German staggered, his left arm waving, and I squared around him and took him clean. The rapier trembled in my hand, appearing magically blood-red between his shoulder blades, and he fell, wrenching the slim steel from my hand.

As I recovered the rapier and turned once more for the summit of the hill, the North Cork began the retreat that ended in their decimation. Rank upon rank of the militia were flooding down the green slopes, their horses galloping before them. And behind them came the rebels with their pikes. In the midst of them was Father John, gigantic in strength, with a pike held high. The North Cork were doomed. Their attack broken on the spears, the reins of their mounts cut by pike slashes, pursued by musket volleys that took them in the back, they went pell-mell. Pausing at times to form themselves into little fight-

ing squares, they were broken again and again by
the onrush of the victorious rebels—surrounded, im-
paled, and pulled down at odds of ten to one. I saw
the German dragoons bunched together at the foot of
the hill, and at the shouted command of Colonel
Foote of the North Cork cavalry, they attempted one
last charge. But the pikes went up like a forest and
the big cavalry horses ran into them, wailing like
injured children.

Leaping across Mia's back, I joined the last charge
down the hill, and in a welter of swinging hoofs and
struggling men, led the pikes into their last, ghastly
business. In moments it was over. The cavalry broke;
the last few survivors staggered in a broken, swaying
line down the escape road to Wexford.

Blood-stained, sickened with the carnage of it, I
led the rebel vanguard down the last slope of Oulart
Hill, and stood among the dead and wounded, listening to Father John's prayer of thanks. For of the
hundred or so militia who had stormed Oulart, more
than ninety were stretched dead in the heather,
while we had lost some fifty dead and another hundred wounded.

It was the first real rebel victory of the rebellion.

Father John cried, his arms high, "The wounded,
including the enemy, will be succored, the dying
given last rites, the dead buried, for we are not

heathen dervishes, we are the soldiers of God. On, on! This is the first victory, and it will raise the country. On, follow me to Carrigroe!"

They thronged about him, they knelt, kissing the hem of his cloth, and one cried, "Camolin first, Father—to capture the guns. For I'm sick to death of shooting wi' a pike!"

"Where is your discipline?" the priest roared back. "Know one thing only—that we are carrying the Cross of Christ!" And he lifted high the great crucifix, shouting, "On, then, to Carrigroe Hill!"

The shout was taken up by thousands of throats and echoed over the hill.

"Carrigroe, *Carrigroe!*"

Attack!

At dawn next day, after camping on Carrigroe, we marched on Camolin and the place was happy to receive us, with the devil loyalists belly-flopping over the hedges to escape the sight of the crucifix we carried. People were out in their nightshirts and hanging out of windows, waving and cheering, and green was everywhere. Green bed-sheets fluttered from poles, and never before in my life have I seen green bed-sheets; green striped tablecloths were being waved in the streets, with the maidens coming up and kissing us with sprigs of May green in their hair. Great was the jubilation, for the rebellion had started and we were top dogs at last. True, a few loyalist militia fought in the middle of the town, but the terrible pikes got among them.

"Arms! Pistols and muskets, Father!" The rebels battered down the door of the arsenal and the little square cannon were trundled out. Muskets and bayonets were piled in the streets for the taking, and the rabble about me did jigs around the piles with their women, the ragged hags of Ferns who had come to greet us.

And Father John cried in the street, "We are the soldiers of God! See, has He not provided us with the tools of conflict? On, on to Enniscorthy, but first to Ferns!"

With the rebel ranks swelling every minute, we formed up to his command.

"Ferns and Enniscorthy!" The frantic cry went round. Banners were hoisted among the marching army, now some eight thousand strong. And when the word flew over the countryside that we were armed with the muskets and cannon of the Camolin arsenal, we were joined by many who owned their own horses and guns—the rebel sons of peasant farmers. The men of Shilmalier came flocking in from the coast—these, the great marksmen who shot the sea birds for sale in Dublin market. And these experts ran up and down the rebel army, teaching men to load and fire the captured muskets. So we marched on Ferns, with waving banners, with bullets whistling through the trees that lined the road, and the women camp-followers jigging and prancing either side of us, waving their rebel-green scarves and kicking up their drumstick legs.

Heaven help us, I thought, if the red-breasted dragoons of England got among us now, for rumor had it that they had already sailed from Fishguard in southwest Wales and would march north to bring us to defeat.

"Regan, are ye there?"

It was the voice of Father John, and I instantly spurred Mia out of the crush and galloped to the front of the farmer cavalry. Fine indeed looked Father John that May morning, gigantic in his long, black gown, with the tall crucifix all glittering in the sun.

As I reached him a rebel spy, dressed in the uniform of the German Hompesch, swung himself into the saddle and galloped away toward Enniscorthy. Father John said, "You mind that ye told me you had important news about Lord Kingsborough? Well, I've just had word from Ennis from Caine Adams, leader of rebel intelligence—you know Joe Lehane of Rudd's Inn, I understand?"

"I do, Father."

"So do I, and a fine fighting man he is, for all his

five-foot size. You shared the secret with Joe, it seems?"

"I did, for you had no time to spare for it in Boolavogue."

"You were right. And little Joe was the right man to tell. He saw the importance of it and passed it on to Caine Adams. You're in big and important company now, son, for Caine Adams himself wants to see ye."

My heart began to thud with joy. My father had been high in the movement of the United Irishmen, but even he had spoken with pent breath of Caine Adams—the man who, next to Wolfe Tone, was the most wanted rebel in Ireland.

Father John continued, "But you'll serve me first, for Enniscorthy is crowded with Protestant fanatics, and they'll kill us to the last man and woman if we fail at the Duffry Gate. And if we don't take Ennis we'll have no need of Lord Kingsborough as a hostage, for we'll be too busy digging our graves. Can ye hear me above this palaver?"

"Yes, Father." This, I thought bitterly, could easily turn into a religious war—Catholic against Protestant.

"So if we win at Ennis you can seek out Caine Adams in the town, but I'll tell ye this now, son. The taking of a hostage is an important business, and if

I had my way I'd send a seasoned soldier, not a callow youth."

"Lord Fitzgerald himself sent me to you," I said.

"That's the sole reason I'm considering you for the job. You know Adams?"

"No, but I know he's a United Irishman of Ennis."

He nodded. "Is he now? Well, you'll have to forgive me, but I'm not so taken with the performances of the society that I'd stake me life on them—they've a wonderful capacity for arriving in the wrong places at the wrong times."

This angered me. "It's untrue! My father was a United Irishman since '91 in the Belfast founding, and Adams served with him, Emmet and O'Connor on the Supreme Executive!"

"Aye, forgive me, lad," he replied. "But you'll have to take a bit of leg-pull on it, you see. For last month your secret society numbered a quarter of a million men, but when it comes to defying the Crown and seizing the land, old Ireland's dependent on a few thousand peasants like this lot—can you see the irony of it?"

I did not reply to this, and he said, "But enough of squabbling, for we'll have a tub o' that before we're finished." He sighed deeply. "I'll let you go to Adams for instructions because you're the son of your father, and because Lord Fitzgerald sent you to me; but I'm telling you this, Regan—I'll brook no mistakes, I'll accept no excuses. You'll hand us the hostage he has in mind, or, by God, you'll have me to answer to, because if I had my way I'd be sending a professional fighter. You're getting the job on the record of your father."

We marched on, silent, and then I said, "Father, do you see this thing?" I took out the little locket that had belonged to the twelve-year-old rebel. "A wee chap who fought for Father Patrick handed me this before he died. If anything happens to me during the journey for Adams, will you give it to his mother in Ennis—his father's name and address are inside."

"Aye, son," said he, and put it in his pocket.

Men and women were lying dead in the streets as we marched through Ferns to the beat of a funeral drum. Father John, carrying the cross with one hand, made a fist of the other and put it against his face, his head bowed as we passed the bodies, and wept.

At the junction of the road to Enniscorthy we stopped and the weary, ragged soldiers flung themselves down to rest. But instantly the Shilmalier sharpshooters were among them, pulling men to their feet for lessons in the use of muskets. And some peasants fell again in hunger. After a bit a group came up to Father John, who was leaning on his cross, and they cried, "We starve, Father!"

A few went on their knees before him, their skinny arms outstretched, their rags fluttering in the hot wind.

"Isn't it the truth ye can catch the musket balls in ye fingers, Father?"

"It is not true," said he.

"But I saw ye up on Oulart, and the bayonets of the North Cork were stabbin' right through ye, sir!"

"That is not true either."

"Give us food, Father John!"

"Make the miracle o' the bread and fishes!"

"Just lift your hands, Holy Father, and the manna'll fall."

He turned from them, staring at the sky. They begged, they pleaded, they kissed the hem of his gown, and he did not turn to them, but said aloud, as if to God, "The manna lies beyond the Duffry Gate. The barns are full in Enniscorthy! All ye need is trust in the Almighty. I am a priest, would ye make me a magician? Away wi' ye! The answer to your prayers lies in Enniscorthy, and God make you worthy of your need."

Raising the cross, he trudged on, and the weary army clambered up and followed him, with the farmer cavalry jogging along at its flank.

Within sight of the spire of Enniscorthy we stopped again, and Father John cried, "Cavalry forward!"

The brawny young farmers galloped before him, reining in, clattering and clanking as they drew their sabers.

"You will cross the river here and enter the town from the other side, blocking the road to Wexford. Take the square beyond the Shannon Quay. We will attack them through the Duffry Gate and fight into Main and Irish streets, can ye hear me?"

"Aye, aye!" the roar went up.

He shouted, "Keep clear o' the castle west of the square, for they've gunned it with artillery, and they'll blow ye back over the Slaney! Are ye ready, men?"

"Ready, Father, ready!"

"Then God go with ye. You're all committed, remember, it's death or victory. *Regan!*"

"Yes, Father?"

"Go with the cavalry but keep to the rear. Michael Green—bide ye a moment!"

A young farmer with a wand of green in his helmet, the leader of the cavalry, reined up his horse. "Aye, sir?"

"Keep this young 'un behind ye, for I want him in on no heroics. He's meeting a United man at the Falcon Inn, d'you know it?"

"On Court Street, Father!"

"Right, you point him to it. Away now, *away!*"

With the young farmer leading, we scrambled down the bank of the Slaney and plunged the horses in, swimming silently for the east bank and the road that cut off any retreat to Wexford.

I looked back once as the vast army approached the Duffry Gate. To my astonishment, I saw the gates swing open and the garrison of Enniscorthy rush out to meet them in a head-on clash of pikes and musket fire. Even across the river we could hear the screams of the wounded men and the camp-followers: hags, perhaps, but many gave their lives at Enniscorthy.

Within five minutes, they told me later, the beautiful Mother Slaney was stained deep red.

The Blind Man of
Enniscorthy

With Mike Green leading, we galloped along the road and I breathed a prayer for Kathleen and Joe Lehane as we thundered past Rudd's Inn. I reckoned it was occupied by the loyalists, for their cavalry yeomen were milling around on the bridge opposite and a few musket balls came winging our way from an upstairs window.

Past the foot of the Enniscorthy bridge we went, and you could see the surprised faces of the loyalist cavalry, for they expected a head-on charge.

"On, on—keep goin'!" It was Mike Green's voice, and I stood up in the stirrups and saw him ten horses ahead, his sword waving. Town deserters, yeomen, and militia were taking running dives into the Slaney as we got among them, and others were flattening in the hedges, yelling like women.

"Are they following, Regan?" bawled Michael Green.

"They are not!" I shouted back.

"Right, then—into the river an' we'll take the far bank!" He swept down the bank and plunged his horse in, and we followed. As Mia began the swim I saw to my right the loyalist cavalry streaming off the bridge and coming after us, sabers flashing.

"They're coming now, Mike," I yelled, "and they're after spilling blood!"

"They're coming too late, son," called the leader. "Once on the town bank we'll be spilling a bit o' theirs," and he floundered out of the shallows and up the slope and threw himself down on the grass. He began to prime a musket, with the rest following his example.

"Regan—off that nag and down flat with ye!"

I obeyed, and Mia went flat beside me, giving me cover.

"Ten sovereigns for that mare if we get out of this alive!" yelled a beefy farmer, taking aim. "The thing's half human!"

"Don't insult the animal," said Michael Green. "*Fire!*"

Sickened, I turned away my face. For the loyalist cavalry took it point-blank, men and horses falling in a heaving, tumbling mass. With a stupid, defiant courage they came on still, sitting targets to the Shilmalier men, the finest shots in the whole of Ireland. They dropped like wheat to the scythe, these horsemen, and the Slaney took them in the flood. Men and horses floundered and cartwheeled, rising once or twice as the current bore them back to the bridge, at last sinking from sight. Michael Green blew the smoke from the barrel of his fowling gun and rose. We had not suffered a single casualty.

"That'll teach them to be loyalists," he said. "Now away wi' us into the town to back up Father John," and he swung himself over his stallion and galloped away over the fields.

Flushing out a cluster of snipers from the roofs of the warehouses, we crawled along the edge of Abbey Quay, leading our horses behind us, and swept the bridge with our musket fire, the Shilmalier men sharpshooting from behind trees. I pitied the loyalist defenders on the bridge for they were packed there like herrings in a barrel as the rebels stormed ten-deep against them with slashing pikes and swords.

"By the saints, look!" shouted Mike Green beside me.

And there came then, in quick, hot flushes of the

wind, a great bellowing and hoarse shouts, and I saw
the heads of horses bobbing among the surrounded
loyalists, with men staggering and falling under the
trampling hoofs.

"Look! It's Father John borrowing the tricks of
Strongbow!"

"He's driving the horses among 'em!"

"Hold fire against the bridge!"

Suddenly there came another rush of horses along
Island Street and I saw the rebel green of the pike-
men goading the poor creatures on from behind. And
the ranks of the loyalists broke here, with the horses
streaming through and the rebels packing in behind
them, splitting the enemy in two.

"Sure, the Holy Father's a man o' war!" cried a
farmer. "By heaven, I never would have believed it!"

"Give him covering fire!"

"Down, men, down!"

And about me the muskets and fowling pieces of
the farmers thundered over the quay. Again and again
they fired, and rank after rank of loyalists flung up
their hands or slipped from sight. On the bridge they
broke and fled, and I saw them falling in swathes before Rudd's Inn, for the rebels held it now and were
spurting fire from every window. The road to Wexford was crammed with fleeing men, but they were
making a last stand in the market place. Great fires

were burning in the town now and smoke was billowing over the sun. Slowly the battle moved up the narrow streets of the town. Rebels were on the bridge and packing themselves up Irish Street as we reached it, and the square was a shambles, rebel and loyalist troops lying in grotesque attitudes of death, and maddened horses stampeding over the cobbles, trampling dead and wounded alike. From almost every window fluttered either the rebel green or the ribbons of the Protestant Orangemen as we galloped through, seeking Father John. Dismounted now, we went from house to house, kicking open doors and prodding out hiding loyalists on the ends of our swords and bayonets. And then, to my joy, I saw Father John himself, standing in the middle of the square, his cross held high.

"You, Regan, gather yourself!" It was Michael Green's voice.

"Here, sir!"

"Away to the Falcon, or you'll never hear the end of it!"

"Right, sir!"

"At the top there!" His horse prancing on the cobbles, he pointed with his pistol, reining in a circle. "Near the corner of Court Street and Spital, away now!"

I took Mia at a walk through the thronged rebels

in the square, amid thunderous cheering and stamping at their great victory. In three hours or less they had taken Enniscorthy and jubilation was in them. Boughs of rebel green were waving everywhere, people were coming up from the cellars cheering the victors, and little children scampered among the troops. But no less than three hundred dead lay in the streets of the town; the cost to us alone was three officers and eighty of the ranks, many of them women.

"Father John, Father John, Father John!" The bloodstained peasants took up the chant, their pikes, muskets, and scythes waving in a forest about him. Pushing Mia gently through them, I gained the corner of Court Street and almost immediately saw the sign of the Falcon Inn. Dismounting, I tethered Mia to a ringbolt, looking up and down the deserted street.

Nothing moved in that street: it was an alley on the edge of the dead. Smoke drifted down, for the defenders had fired a couple of hundred houses before their retreat, and I could hear the clashing of pails and buckets. But Spital and Court were as quiet as midnight vaults, and I saw Mia rolling her eyes white, always a sign of the unearthly.

Drawing my little pistol, I turned the handle of the inn door and pushed it open with a creak.

A man was sitting at a bench in the taproom. Like

some Biblical patriarch he looked sitting there, with his fine white hair flowing over his shoulders and his black robes and his face stark white and smooth, like a man embalmed. I knew him instantly from my father's description: Caine Adams, the unfrocked priest of Enniscorthy, once a churchman Protestant, now a leader of the United Irishmen.

"Is that you, Regan?" His voice was a whisper and his eyes moved strangely blue in the marble smoothness of his face, and at once I knew him for blind.

"It is me, John Regan, sir," I said. "Are you Caine Adams?"

"Move your hand before my face and get the proof of it," said he.

With horror I remembered my father's words: the Hessians had held him over a forge and struck the red iron, and the sparks had seared his eyes.

He said curtly, "Now shut the door and face me, and give me the proof of you."

"My father was Sean Regan of Milford. He served with Lawless and O'Connor and knew the house of Sweetman," I said.

His face did not change, but he said quietly, "Together we once ate in Sweetman's house. Your father is dead, they tell me—my soul is with him. He had a fine big mare, but her name escapes me." I knew he was still testing me.

"Mia."

Suddenly, reaching out, he ran his ice-cold fingers over my face, pausing on every feature, and I shivered before those sightless eyes as his hand dropped to my throat.

"You've the Regan head on ye," said he at length. "God pray you keep it on your shoulders in the cause of Ireland. D'you know the landlord of Rudd's Inn?"

"Aye, indeed!"

"His name, then."

"Joseph Lehane, and his daughter's name is Kathleen."

"It's a fair beginning," said he, and smiled, "for they tell me she's winsome. It was Joe Lehane who recommended you, did you know that?"

"And Father John had no hand in it?" I asked, though in my heart I knew the truth.

"Father John thought ye too young for the task in mind, though ye came from Lord Fitzgerald; but Joe Lehane had the last word on it. However, you'll be answering to Father John in the outcome, d'you realize that?"

"Aye, he told me."

"And I'd not be standing in your boots if ye fail him, remember." He added softly, "Take me congratulations for starting this thing, Regan, but now you've started it you've got to finish it. Lehane told me that you took the Dublin headquarters' letter to Kingsborough himself, and gave it to him in person."

"I did, sir."

"Did he ask your name?"

"He did."

"Lehane tells me you stayed at Rudd's Inn some five months back with your father—did Kingsborough see you then?"

"No, sir."

"I hope you're right because he's a wonderful memory for faces—to say nothing of ye being the spit and image of your dead father, according to Joe."

I said, "Lord Kingsborough did ask if I had relatives serving under him because my name and face seemed familiar."

"Och, that's it!" whispered Adams. "He's as cagey as a wagon of monkeys, that one. If I'm using you to catch his lordship I'd best keep ye out o' his sight until the death, so to speak."

"The death?"

The blind man chuckled softly. "It's you or Kingsborough, son, and if he gets another sight o' your face, it'll more than likely be you. Are ye ready to take this chance? For he's no fool, is this one."

"Of course I'll take it."

"Good." He rose unsteadily, hand out, feeling for things. "Is the place shut fast, son?"

"Aye."

"I have ears that hear brown grass growin'—it's only me eyes, ye understand." He leaned over the table, his face an inch from mine. "Now, listen. We've not been sleeping since you reported to Joe Lehane, and we've just had news back that Kingsborough's officer, a Captain Bourke, has been down the coast at Mizen Head to commission a ketch to take the great fella in secret to Wexford."

"So he *is* going!" I exclaimed.

"He's not only going, son, but Joe Lehane is taking him, for it just so happened that little Joe and Kathleen were sailing their ketch into Mizen when Captain Bourke arrived!"

"Just so happened, eh!" I grinned at his sightless face.

"That's the way of good intelligence. The timing is just as important as the execution of the plan. And Bourke jumped at it, of course, for as far as the North Cork are concerned, little Joe is a trusted man."

In admiration I thumped my fist into my palm. "Och, there's no flies on Joe Lehane—my father used to say that."

"And there's none on Kingsborough either." Caine Adams reached out and gripped my wrist. "He'll not be traveling alone, for all the fact he reckons he's in safe company. Bourke is with him, and another escort

officer, one of the Hompesch Germans. But more—
there's a rough Irish character called Patrick Hays in
the pay of the North Cork, an' he's down in Wexford
this minute, waiting to ride to Mizen Head to say if
the town is free."

"And if it is rebel occupied?"

Caine Adams replied, "If it is rebel threatened,
Hays will ride to Mizen Head and warn Lord Kingsborough not to sail." He sighed. "A truebred Irishman, is it? This Patrick Hays has been in the pay of
the North Cork for months—he's the dirt under the
feet of decent people."

Faintly, I heard the crackle of muskets as loyalist
militia and yeomen remnants were flushed out of the
town by the victorious rebels.

Adams said, "Are ye listening, son?"

"I am, sir."

"Right. Now, at this moment Joe Lehane and his
daughter Kathleen are in their fishing smack at Mizen
Head, waiting to carry Kingsborough's party to Wexford, as I told you. They have been commissioned by
Kingsborough himself, and he welcomed little Joe
with open arms for the trip, for he's a trusted man.
Are ye with me?"

"Yes."

"But Patrick Hays may not be a trusted man, for
nobody on earth, including Lord Kingsborough, can

truly trust an informer. So even if Hays reports a rebel occupation, he may sail for Wexford just the same—and cruise off the coast to get the feel of things, you understand?"

"I do, sir."

"On the other hand, Kingsborough's no fool, and he might become suspicious. And if he becomes too suspicious he might arrest Joe and Kathleen, in case they're implicated in the plot to get him to Wexford and in the hands of Father John. And ye know what that means, don't you?"

I did not reply, and he lowered his voice, saying, "It means the rope for the pair of them if the truth comes out, but it means terror for young Kathleen. Have ye heard what happens to young women in the hands of the Hompesch?" I bowed my head, and he must have sensed my disgust, for he said, "So it's up to you. Your job is to protect the Lehanes—leave Patrick Hays to me."

"What—what do you want of me?" I asked.

"I want you to track Patrick Hays. At this moment he's in the Parrot Inn in Wexford town. The landlord is a good United Irishman—a bald, fat fella with no name as far as you're concerned—and he's sent word that Hays is staying there. And for sure he's waiting to see which way the wind blows—if Father John marches on Newtownbarry next, or Wexford.

And the moment he knows it's Wexford, Hays'll be off to Mizen Head to give warning to Kingsborough."

"You just want me to track him?"

"Track him from the moment he leaves the town. Stay with him, be his shadow. Stay stitched to him—but don't let him get wind of ye—until you're sure he's riding to Mizen. And the moment you're certain of this, go like the wind down to the bay and warn Joe Lehane. Tell him to set sail if there's any sign that a North Cork troop is coming to arrest him. Sail with him if Kingsborough comes."

"You want me to protect the Lehanes."

"That and no more, for they're sitting ducks at the moment, and we've got to protect our people. I can think of no better job for ye, son, for Joe was your father's friend."

"And Hays gets away?" I asked.

He lit his pipe and the smoke flowered between us, and his face, stark white and lined with age, wavered like something disembodied in the stuttering light of the match. He said, "And Hays gets away—as far as you're concerned—for the man is my property. You understand that?"

"Yes, sir."

"Then remember it. Touch a hair of his head, delay him in any way, and you'll not have to account to me.

You'll account to the Rebel Committee sitting in Wexford, and you know what that means?"

Sweat was on my face. I got up from the table.

Adams said, "Now get some sleep for a couple of hours while I keep watch. For you're off before dawn to Wexford, and may God go with ye."

"Yes," I replied.

"And may God help ye, son, if you let Patrick Hays out of your sight." He added, "Even at the cost of losing Kingsborough you'll get Joe and his girl back to Wexford safe and sound, you understand?"

"Yes, sir."

"And no heroics—just do that and nothing more, for I know you young hotheads. Anyway, you tangle with Patrick Hays and he'll lay you down and draw the bones from your back, for he's a hard-nut professional."

"Yes, sir," I said.

The Parrot Inn

After dousing the fires and searching the town of Enniscorthy for arms and ammunition, Father John garrisoned the place and led his main force of victorious rebels up to the summit of Vinegar Hill, by the windmill that overlooks the land. Soon the hill was dotted with campfires, and there was a smell of cook-pots simmering in the wind as the rebels fed. As for me, I downed half a basin of rabbit pie given me by the landlady of the Falcon, put an outsize bag of oats on Mia, and slept while Caine Adams sat guard over me in the taproom, and when I awoke under his hand three hours later it was still dark. I changed into the peasant clothes he gave me.

"Repeat the password," said he.

"Wexfree," I said, sitting up.

"Aye—*Wexfree*, or you'll never get out of the town alive. Now, tell me—the name of the inn you go to in Wexford?"

"The Parrot." I tied on a rebel-green scarf.

"Right—and the landlord?"

"A little fat chap with a big paunch and a bald head, but no name."

"Right again. Now listen. A messenger of the rebel cavalry came last night with this." He gave me a packet. "Father John himself sent it with orders that you hand it to the landlord of the Parrot—no questions asked, no answers given. Just hand it to him in private, understand?"

Mounting Mia, I left Caine Adams then. Out of the town we went, away from the bonfire that once was lovely Enniscorthy, and on the banks of the Slaney they were burying the dead, for I heard the chink of the shovels.

A hag-ridden witch of a night this proved to be, with the wind gusting in the glowering trees above us, and little screechings coming from the wayside thickets where stoats were hunting. And I knew, as I spurred Mia into a gallop, that hidden loyalists and deserters were watching me from the hedges, men who would shoot in the back for the price of a horse. After a bit I began to sweat at the thought of this, so I leaped the road hedge and we took over the fields to Oylgate.

Now there was a great love in me for the big, gray mare who had first linked her life with my father and was now putting her trust in me, and I cried to her above the howling of the wind, "Faster, faster! The mares of Satan are after ye!" And at this she tossed her mane, and I reached forward and gripped it with both hands, pulling hard, and shouting again, "Mia, Mia, *Mia!*" She neighed reply at the full stretch of her gallop, loving it, and there came to me a sudden sense of cleanness, for all the killings and cruelties had been washed away by the love of this companion.

If the Man in the Big Seat calls me at last to the gates of heaven and I find no horses stabled there, I'm having a personal word with St. Peter on the subject.

Beyond Promontory Fort I pulled off my rebel-green scarf and stuffed it under Mia's saddle, for wounded loyalists were flocking along the road. Later I dismounted and jostled Mia in among them, becoming a horse and rider just escaped from Enniscorthy. West of the Wexford town-square the loyalist cavalry were out; with a group of rebel prisoners they were driving up to the gaol, and they called, "Is it true that Ennis is taken?"

"Every street, every house—and in three hours' fighting!"

"And that the rebels are plundering and burning the place?"

A man beside me yelled, "An' killing women and childer, for I saw it with my own eyes!" And I swear he had never seen the skies over Ennis while the battle was on.

"They're killing the prisoners!"

"And drowning the children in the Slaney!"

Like a prairie fire the panic and rumors spread. Women in their night clothes were running through the streets.

"They put the place to the sword, on the orders of Father John Murphy!"

An old woman knelt beside me as I marched with the crowd of refugees, and she pulled her hair over her face in grief and cried, "Holy God be with us, for there's a great evil spreadin' among us!"

"And now they're marching on Wexford!"

"They are not," I cried, "for I have just got out of Ennis!"

"Where are they marching next, then?" asked a soldier, and he looked to me like one of the North Cork who fought on Oulart Hill.

I said, "The rumors are saying they're going north for Newtownbarry!"

"Is that a fact?"

A crowd of people, joyous now, danced about me.

Because I had a horse they were directing their attention to me, and it was becoming dangerous. A cavalry officer of the Donegal Militia clattered up, and this surprised me, for I didn't know they were within a hundred miles of Wexford.

"How do ye know it's Newtownbarry, then?" he shouted.

"There's wounded rebels talking of it." And to my relief and surprise he shouted his thanks and galloped past us.

In the town the people were milling about and women and children shouting about how the rebels were coming to kill and burn, and most of the ships anchored along the quay were thronged with people begging the captains to make an escape. Tables had been pulled out of the houses and the town square was a bedlam of industry, with every spare man in the place blowing up forges to fashion pike-heads for the defense, and cannon being dragged over the cobbles toward the Promontory Fort to guard the road to Enniscorthy. Men, women, and children were grabbing anything that would float and jumping into the sea and paddling themselves to ships at anchor. Never in my life had I seen such panic.

"It's the Catholic army comin'!"

"And the Protestants will be slaughtered to a man!"

And on every side men and women were accosting Catholic priests, asking them to sign bits of paper certifying that they had been good friends to the Catholics, or even, in many cases, saying that they had changed their religion.

"The town is going mad!" shouted a man.

"What ails you people?" yelled another. "Sure to heaven, there's as many Protestants as Catholics in the army of Father Murphy!"

But it was no good telling them this. From every window the colored ribbons of the Protestants were being hauled in and flags of green taking their place, and groups of people of all denominations in Wexford were on their knees in the side streets, praying shoulder to shoulder to the same sweet God.

Away from the shouts and prayers I found a quiet place off Keysers Lane and there we rested, Mia and I, until the first faint tinges of dawn fingered the sea. I was desolate in spirit. Our rebel cause was already being split apart. The people of Wexford were terrified that what had begun as a war against English oppression would end in a religious bloodbath.

Only when the sun came up did I stroll with Mia through the back streets to the Parrot Inn, which lay just off Corn Market. I thought, as I led her through the throngs of people standing there, of the other terror over a century ago when the beast Cromwell gathered every citizen of Wexford in that little cobbled market—men, women, and helpless little children—for his Roundheads to put to the sword.

There was in me a great compassion for these little people of Wexford as I led Mia into the stable yard of the Parrot.

"Stabling and a meal, lad?" asked the landlord, coming out. He was wearing a blue apron and was potted in the stomach and heavy in the jowls.

"If you please," I said.

"You're safe with me," said he, taking Mia's bridle. "I'm as good a Catholic as Father John Murphy would wish."

"It makes no odds," I said.

He shrugged his fat little shoulders. "But to be on the safe side I've a paper from me priest, certifying I took the Holy Mass. One and sixpence a night suit you?"

"Aye,"

He stabled Mia and came back, which gave me the chance to look the place over. If Caine Adams had not sent me to this inn, I would have said it looked innocent enough.

"When d'you think he's like to arrive, then?" asked the landlord.

"Who?" I asked, playing for time, for a man was

standing by the window of the taproom, and I could almost hear him listening.

"Father John and the rebels?"

"Never, more than likely," I answered.

"But the town's in a panic, don't ye know? They're rigging up roadblocks and making pikes. The townspeople are calling up General Fawcett himself and the Donegal Militia, and they're on their way this moment to Duncannon Fort!"

"They're wasting their time," I said loudly. "Wexford's too big a nut for the priest to crack. They're marching north, to Newtownbarry."

He stared at me, his face coming alight with relief and joy. "But how d'you know all this, son?"

"Because I was about the last loyalist out of Enniscorthy—I got out by the skin o' me teeth. The priest has got them out in the streets. At first light—about now—he'll be marching on Newtownbarry."

"God be praised!" He turned from me, calling, "Ginny, me girl—d'you hear it? Mr. Hays, sir—did ye hear the news the boy brings?"

A little dumpling of a woman came rushing into the yard, her hands clasped in relief. A shadow moved on the glass of the taproom and a big man followed her and leaned against the yard door.

The landlord cried, "The lad here has just come in from Ennis. The rebels are marching on Newtownbarry—they're not laying a hand on Wexford!"

His wife closed her eyes and turned her face to the dawn, lips moving in a soundless prayer.

"Isn't it wonderful news?" shouted the landlord. "Did you hear, Mr. Hays?"

"It's good news indeed," said the man called Hays. He bowed stiffly toward me.

I bowed back to him. "Good morning," I said.

And I gave a fleeting thought of thanks to Caine Adams. Despite the fact that the leaders of the United Irishmen were scattered on the wind, the blind man of Enniscorthy could see to the very kernel of the nut.

I gave the man Hays a grin as I pushed past him into the taproom.

Aye yes, this was the most important house in Wexford right enough.

Later I got the proof of it.

Making sure that the little landlord was alone in the taproom, I wandered in and called for a pewter of home-brew, and when he served me with it I placed on the counter before him the little packet Caine Adams had given me.

"A present from Enniscorthy," and I stared past him through the window.

The landlord's expression did not change as he dropped it into his pocket.

"Much obliged," he said.

The Mad Woman of Gorey

I slept for only two hours that morning and awoke
to the sounds of great rejoicing. Pulling on my clothes,
I ran downstairs, through the taproom and into the
street, and saw in passing that the horse of the man
called Hays was still stabled next to Mia. Indeed,
Hays was out on the quay when I got there, and I
saw for the first time the fine size and build on him.
I saw too that he had a rapier of the Dublin school
girded on him, which was proof to anyone that he
was no fool with it. But he cried like a schoolboy with
excitement when I reached him, "It's a procession
comin'! An' in the name of St. Peter it's a fine and
grand one!"

I pushed my way to the water's edge, for the crowd was thickening with folks running from their houses with loud hurrahs. Gone was the terror of yesterday.

"What's the procession for?" I asked.

"It's Bagenal Harvey and John Colclough released from the gaol!" cried a man. "And look—there's Edward Fitzgerald, the squire, coming with 'em!"

"Och, you're daft, man!" shouted a woman. "Didn't Lord Edward get attacked and wounded, and isn't he lying this moment in a Dublin gaol?"

"Och, girl," cried Hays testily, "it's not the same fella. But the way this lot's goin' they'll end up just the same!"

I glanced at Patrick Hays. Big and handsome he looked, with the sun bright on his yellow hair, and I saw on his cheeks the crisscross scars of the rapier expert, the telltale evidence of his trade—the professional fighter. And he moved with the same feline grace I had seen before in born killers. Strangely, his face, and especially his voice, seemed faintly familiar, though I was sure I had never seen him before.

Now the chattering, excited crowd was packing itself along the quay, for the procession was coming, headed by fiddlers and a dancing bear on a chain. Gypsy Irish were banging on tambourines, and it was a gay sight, all splashed and gaudy in red and rebel greens.

"Bagenal Harvey! Bagenal Harvey!" The crowd

took up the chant and I shouldered people aside to catch a glimpse of this new hero. This was the Protestant landowner who had been betrayed to the Irish Parliament; now he had been released from Wexford gaol by the rebels. I expected to see a giant; instead I saw a man inches shorter than I.

"Bagenal Harvey! Bagenal Harvey!" The crowd roared the name of the new leader who had taken the reins from the wounded Fitzgerald, the man of destiny who they prayed would lead their country to freedom. Perhaps, because of his stature and command, he might be able to hold in check a Catholic army of ragged rebels already drunk with power. A friend of Father Murphy, he was loved by men of all denominations and hated by the English aristocracy.

Small he was, but as he came to the head of the procession his dignity and serenity of countenance lent him gigantic size and strength. And as he drew abreast of me the little old landlord of the Parrot cried, "Have ye heard the latest, son? Bagenal Harvey is off to Ennis to draw up a bargain with Father Murphy!" He did a little jig of delight and the people pressed about us in smells of hot cloth and sun.

"What sort of bargain?" demanded Hays, beside me.

"Didn't ye hear the town crier, man? The pair of them are offering safe conduct and amnesty to the

rebels if they'll throw down their arms and disperse
—the town is safe, don't ye see?"

I gave a secret grin. The little landlord was pretty
good, I thought, at playing the twin roles of liar and
fool.

Hays said, moodily, "Murphy won't disperse,
landlord. He's got the bit between his teeth now, and
he won't disarm for the King of England himself.
Only force will bring him down."

"At Newtownbarry," I said.

Hays nodded, raising his voice above the cheering
people. "You're probably right—at Newtownbarry.
If he captured that the road would be open to Wicklow and the north."

The little landlord crossed himself. "God spare
us . . ."

"But he won't get Newtownbarry," I said. "Colonel L'Estrange and his militia will cut that lot to
pieces."

"Rebel swine," breathed Hays.

Cheerfully, I patted the landlord's shoulder. "Either
way, you're safe in Wexford. Bagenal Harvey's runnin' this town now, not Father John Murphy."

"The lad's right, landlord, so rest in peace," said
Hays, and looked at his watch. "And it's past midday,
so I'd better be off."

"Me, too," I said.

He turned on the pavement. "Which way are ye riding, son?"

"West, sir. I'm bound for Waterford to see me maiden aunt."

"Pity," he remarked. "I'm going north."

I had to grin because I knew this already, and turned away from Patrick Hays, staring at the harbor. Everything was going according to plan, step by step. I was lounging on the sea wall when Patrick Hays called from the road, "Good-by to you."

"Good-by," I said.

I watched him go into the Parrot yard and saw him come out leading a big, brown stallion. He mounted with easy grace and trotted off along the road to Ferrycarrig, breaking into a gallop the moment he thought he was out of sight. I ran inside the Parrot, and the landlord was standing in the taproom as if awaiting me.

He said, "There's no time now for pleasantries, son. Now that he's gone we can talk cleanly. You realize that Father John has started the march and that he'll be in the town in the next twenty-four hours?"

"Yes," I said.

"And ye realize, too, that Patrick Hays knows this —for all his agreeing with you about Newtownbarry being the next to fall?"

"I do."

"Then get after him. Carry out the orders of Caine Adams to the letter. Stay close to him, understand? For if Kingsborough doesn't arrive here and we get no hostage, God help me and my wife, God help Joe Lehane and his daughter."

I protested. "But will Hays tell Kingsborough to come when he knows the town will be occupied within a couple of days?"

He gripped me, staring into my face. "Don't question, lad, just do as you're told. Leave the brains of it to Caine Adams, who has got some."

He led Mia out and held her while I saddled her up with frantic speed, but he didn't release the bridle. In a low, threatening voice, he said, "Don't think, for ye haven't the gumption to work it out. Just stay stitched to Hays, ye understand, or you'll pay with your life for it."

He turned his back on me as I galloped off after Hays.

Beyond Ferrycarrig I led Mia, who was limping, into a cool glade, and here she lifted one of her forelegs to me and stared as if in mute apology, so I patted the grass before her and she went flat for me. It was a lucky one—a little flint lodged under her shoe—and I had it out in a jiffy. Immediately she was up on her feet, walking around trying her weight on it as old-fashioned as you like, and then she trotted over and nuzzled me for thanks.

"Right," I said, "now no more messin'—get after that stallion, for we're supposed to keep the fella in sight," and we swung out of the glade and took the coast road to Blackwater. But although Mia stretched it out, with the froth lying on her neck, we had lost good time. I reckoned Hays was more than five miles ahead now, five miles that might mean life or death to Joe and Kathleen.

It was late afternoon by the time we reached Ballycanew, and deep dusk when we rode into the outskirts of Gorey. Here, I rested Mia until darkness, for it was rumored that Gorey was in rebel hands, and rebels, at times, could be more dangerous than Hompesch, since they often took a bang at you from a top window just for the fun of it. Also, with the dash after Hays, I had left the Parrot without food, and the sickness of an empty stomach was rising in my throat.

Going at a trot through Gorey was like a stroll in the caverns of the dead. True, the yeomen had retreated, but in their retreat they had burned, plundered, and shot, and the poor dead peasants were lying outside their cottage doors—men, women, and children, their faces stark white in the light of the moon. With all the cabins locked and barred, nothing moved in the once gay little town that was now a cemetery. Half a dozen men—loyalist militia by the look of them—were lying wounded against a wall, and although they did not speak, one raised his fist and cursed me as I passed. I dared not stop to help them, for every minute counted in this ride to Mizen Head. I heard galloping hoofs coming behind me, and I drew Mia into the shadows of an alley and waited, but the sound died on the wind.

And then, suddenly, I heard faint keening, as of an Irish wake, and down the road came a woman in rags and tatters. Mia shuddered under me and backed deeper into the alley as the woman began to dance. Down the middle of the street she danced in her clogs, prancing and wailing, her skinny arms flung up, her bony knees jabbing out. And in that yellow light I saw her face. A ghostly gray it was, with a cackle of a mouth and her stringy hair flying and her eyes all red. Red, red were those eyes, and I shall never forget them. About her I learned later, the mad woman of Gorey, the town that once was so fair.

Now again came the sound of hoofbeats from the opposite direction, and the woman crouched, listening. Then, with a shriek, she ran to the roadside and began to roll a barrel over the cobbles. I rose in the stirrups, staring in wonder. Round and round she rolled the barrel and a blackness was spilling from it. Down on her knees now, she flung the contents high, spraying it over the road, and I shouted at her when I realized it was gunpowder, and started forward, spurring Mia. But Mia was rooted with terror and would not budge, so I slid from the saddle and raced down the road, yelling and waving my arms at the oncoming rider, and the mad woman screamed, "May the devil take ye soul, Patrick Hays! May ye singe on white-hot grids for the foul informer that ye are!"

But there was no time to consider if it was Hays or not, for the rider spurred and came even faster, and I heard the ring of steel as he pulled out his saber. Leaping from his path, I rolled into the roadside gutter, pressing myself flat, and I heard the tip of his blade slash within inches of me as he thundered past. In a moment he was beyond me, the hoofs of his fine black horse sparking on the cobbles. I shouted another warning on my knees, but too late. When he reached the strewn powder, the road blazed. Horse and rider were enveloped in a ball of red fire, and although I was crouching now, the blast of it bowled me over like a piece of paper in the wind. Kneeling in the undergrowth, I stared at the spot where horse and rider had been. Nothing was there. Rising to my feet, I walked unsteadily toward the crater in the road. Smoke billowed up from a gaping hole.

And then, rising from behind a wall, came the tattered, smoke-grimed form of the mad woman of Gorey. Motionless she stood, her head back, her arms flung up in some primeval obeisance to the stars. Then, sensing my presence, she slowly turned, and as if indicting me for her own crime, she croaked, "Now stands ye soul, Patrick Hays, with ye body shattered. And may ye take that soul to hell, Patrick Hays, in the name of the people of Ireland!"

Turning, I fled.

Horrified by this madness, I raced down a nearby alley, shouting for Mia. But she, in equal terror, had galloped to the very edge of the town. There I found her, safe but shivering as with an ague, and I leaped into her saddle.

"Get on, get on!" I cried.

And she didn't need telling twice, for we went like the clappers of Lucifer, streaking through the shambles of Gorey under the cold, gray light of the moon.

Coming down to a trot a mile or so on, I began to wonder if Patrick Hays was dead. If dead he was he had changed horses in the meantime, for the stallion he was riding when he left Wexford was a pretty color of brown.

I didn't stop to consider this further, but kept riding. If I ever see the skies over Gorey again it will be a hundred years too soon.

Ambushed!

They ambushed me on Tara Hill, on the east slope between the summit and Ballymoney, and I cursed myself for a fool because I had been more than half expecting it and, until now, had always kept to the open country. And the way they did it made me think they were militia, for it is the cruelest possible way to ambush a rider. Luckily I was trotting Mia at the time. They strung a rope between two trees, and it took me in the throat, pulling me off backwards. The moment I fell, Mia galloped off in the way she had been trained. I rose from the ground, and in a moment they were about me, rising behind boulders,

hand-dropping from the trees. Half-starved peasantry by their looks, their shattered faces peering at
me in the pale light.

"Well, well," exclaimed one, "the heavens be
praised. The fella is all in one piece for the taking."
His gaunt shoulders shook with laughter. "D'ye
know somethin', soldier? You spoiled the fun. The
trick o' it is to take the rope at speed, and then it
cuts ye in half, which makes it harder on the parish
prayers but easier on the burial." He came nearer,
the rest following him. There were six of them; four
had pikes and one a scythe.

"I am not a militia," I said, my hand to my throat.

"Ah! It can speak—and hoity-toity, too—hark at
it!"

" 'Tis a strange form of Irish, I'm thinking."

"Are ye Irish indeed, me man?" asked another,
pushing his face up to mine.

"Like the shamrock," I replied. "What the hell
are ye doing—ambushing your own kith and kin?"

"Dear me, hark at it!" cried a third. "Are ye telling
us there's no shamrock Irish in the North Cork?"

"The barracks are full of 'em!"

I said evenly, "But they are not Irish."

It stilled them, and they ringed me, and even the
bright moon seemed pitilessly to enhance the poverty
of their scarecrow bodies and work-lined faces.

One cried, "I say string him up and hand him a hundred lashes, just for the joy of it."

"He'd not come even with me, mind—I've had two hundred. Do ye deny you're North Cork, son?"

"I'm rebel green, the same as you," I replied. They were gabbling among themselves, and for this I cursed them more. For I was listening. A little wind blew from the sea, and I thought I heard galloping hoofs; Mia would be back in the next five minutes, as my father had trained her.

Then one said, "If you're rebel green, will ye tell me why you're not wearing it?"

"I was afraid of a loyalist ambush—I have a scarf as green as the hills under my saddle."

One, the biggest, put a pike against my chest. "Have ye money?"

"A bit."

"And a fine sword on ye, unless I'm mistaken." He fingered the hilt of my rapier while the others covered me. "Do ye see the jewels in the handle of it, Doyle? That thing itself would feed the starving of Ballymoney for the next six months." He grinned into my face. "It's a village badly named. They call it Ballymoney, but there's never a shilling to be found in the place, and the children crying for bread, Mr. Hays."

This startled me. Until now I had thought them

to be mere vagabonds, wayside footpads who would capture and strip a man of his every possession. Now I knew them to be of greater importance.

"My name is not Hays," I said.

"Then what is it?"

"John Regan."

The leader said, hands on hips, "Is that a fact? So you deny there's comings and goings between Wexford and the North Cork camp up in Arklow?"

"There probably is, but I'm nothing to do with it."

"Then what are ye doing here?"

"I'm a messenger riding for Father John of Boolavogue."

"Is that so? Father John Murphy who has taken Ennis?"

I nodded.

"Then you must have been given a password, though I'm inclined not to believe ye."

"Wexfree," I said, though I knew it was a waste of time. This was the password Adams had given me, but there was no reason to think they would know it in Ballymoney.

"What in the hell is that supposed to mean?"

"The freeing of Wexford, ye fools!"

"Oh, aye?" They grinned their disbelief.

One of them, coming up behind me, began to unbuckle my rapier.

"Is he armed, Tom?" He added, "For he looks sharp enough for a gun."

The same man ran his hands over my body, and he paused on my little pistol and pulled it out.

I said, "If ye don't know the password you shouldn't be abroad arresting your own kind."

"It's a fine wee pistol, is this one," said the leader, tossing it up. "It'll fetch a shillin' or two in Wicklow market, I'll be bound. Will ye be so good as to turn out your money now, Mr. Hays, before we cut ye down?"

Playing for time, I turned out my pockets, straining my ears for the sound of Mia's returning hoofs. But there was no sound but the wind and the distant crashing of the sea.

The leader said, "Bring the rope, Ben. We'll string up the Christian gentleman the same way the North Cork strung up me son—with a stone under his toe so he can play around wi' it." He turned to me. "He was fifteen years old, and they strung him up this special way, an' shall I tell ye why, Mr. Hays? Because he dived at the legs of a yeoman who was taking a whip to his mother. We've waited you long, man. We've seen you wearing out the flints between here and Wexford, informing on the movements o' your own flesh and blood. D'you think us fools? Isn't it a wonderful coincidence that we happen to be out

tonight just as you ride through to give more in-
formation to Kingsborough?"

"What do you know of Kingsborough?"

"More than ye think, man, but in the place
you're goin' to it won't be considered important."

"You've got the wrong man, and my blood will
be on your heads," I said, desperately. "Are ye that
brutal that you string a fella up before you get the
proof of him? Is this the way you expect to free the
country?"

"Have ye got the string, Mooney?"

"Get his hands tied and finish it, for he's chock
full o' the gab."

I shouted, "There's a fishing smack waiting off
Mizen Head, and a chap there who'll give the proof
that I'm not Hays—I keep telling you, my name is
Regan!"

"*Arrah!*" cried another. "He's a tongue on him like
the serpents of Babylon. They tell me informer's
tongues are six inches longer than the normal. I tell
ye, Sam, he'll still be chattering when he stands before St. Peter, but there'll be nothing in the Book of
Heaven to say a decent word for him!"

One began to tie my hands, and he said, with
hate in his voice, "They've been stringing up the
patriots of Ballymoney and burning us with the pitch
caps. Aye, indeed—guns and pikes are buried in

the village, for we're fine and proud Irishmen. And we'd have risen a month or so before this if it hadn't been for the likes of you, telling us to bide our time in the name of better things to come. But we know the truth of ye now."

I could hear the approach of galloping hoofs, and so could the rebels. The man tying my wrists paused, listening. The one with the rope was about to toss it over a bough above him, but now he held it hard against him.

It was Mia. I could hear her plainly now, the drumming of her hoofs growing louder, louder. Yet it was a strangely new rhythm of hoofbeats, and I was puzzled. Every nerve in me was tingling for the kick and rush for her saddle. Nearer, nearer came the hoofs, and then the snort of a horse laboring up the slope, and I knew suddenly that it was not Mia. Riding at us full pelt the horseman came, straight as an arrow along the track between the trees. And we flung ourselves aside as he plunged among us and I saw his face as I lay in the thick roadside grass. In a moment he was gone, at full gallop down the hill. I got up, and so did the rebels. I made no attempt at escape, although they were off their guard.

"You damned fools," I whispered, "that was the man you want—that was Hays." It was astonishing. I had thought Hays to be ahead of me but I must have passed him in the darkness, for Mia had been traveling at tremendous speed.

Perplexed, they stared at each other, and one said softly, "The boy gives the truth of it. It's Hays right enough, and though I've never seen his face, I know the ride of him."

"On the big brown stallion," said another.

"If ye look hard enough, you'll see mine's a mare," I said, brushing myself down. "Or don't ye know the difference?"

"Dear heaven!" They stared at each other.

"We might 'ave hanged the wrong one!"

I said, "Unless I'm mistaken it's not the first time you've done it, ye blithering fools."

They knelt, they patted and smoothed me, they buckled the rapier back on me, and returned the money and the pistol.

"God speed ye, son, wherever you're going!"

Mia was coming in at a gallop and I threw up my hands to slow her. "He has gained on me," I said, getting into the saddle, "thanks to you."

They stood in a group and doffed their hats and pulled their hair as I left them, and the leader, in a sudden gesture that begged forgiveness, ran alongside Mia and raised his clasped hands to me.

"You kill too easy, man," I said. "Because the heathen rule us, do ye have to behave like heathen?"

"Och, lad, we're only watching over our friends!" he cried.

"Do the likes of you have friends?"

He shouted, "We wanted the truth of Hays, we wanted his purpose. For the North Cork were through the village this morning making enquiries about a fisherman and his daughter who are up in Mizen for service to Kingsborough."

Instantly I reined in. "A fisherman and his daughter?"

"Aye. The big brutal sergeant was checking him out, for he's supposed to be a friend of Kingsborough."

"You know this fisherman?" I asked.

At this the leader rubbed his chin, grinning; the others grinned back.

"I know him, too, and I'm on me way to him now," I said.

"Joe Lehane?"

I nodded, and the man said, "Then go fast on ye nag and tell him this—for all he reckons he's in with the North Cork, Kingsborough's having him checked. It was this big sergeant come, you see, with two others. And they cottoned on to old Tom Haggard, and old Tom gabbled his tongue about Joe, under threat of torture."

"He's half a man, and he gabbled," said another,

viciously. "He told how Joe was a United Irishman."

A sickness was welling up in my throat. "When was this?" I was mentally calculating that Joe and Kathleen, at this moment, might already have been arrested.

"Early this mornin', sir," replied the leader, "but ye needn't worry for Joe. The soldiers got the answer they wanted, but they'll not be reportin' the truth of it to Kingsborough."

I looked down at them and they shifted their feet like scolded children.

"They're down six feet," said the leader.

"You—you murdered them?"

"What else could we do?" He opened his hands to me. "We've got to protect the patriots. Och, sure to God they went swift, an' as easy as a prayer, and we took Tom Haggard along with 'em for good measure, for we canna stomach an informer."

It was incredible. Once peaceful peasants, these men now killed at the drop of a hat: this was the horror that came in the wake of rebellion.

The leader said, "We were away to Mizen to warn Lehane that he's being checked."

"I'll warn Joe and Kathleen," I said, and they brightened at the names. "You make yourselves scarce among the hills of Ballymoney."

I spurred away, consumed with hatred for men

like Patrick Hays and all he stood for. Men such as he, I thought, were responsible for the terror that was stalking my country. Could Caine Adams, from such a distance, measure the evil in this man? If the North Cork suspected Joe, surely Hays did too. The situation, I considered, had changed. I would handle this in my own way.

Only one thought was beating in my brain. I had to stop Patrick Hays from reaching Mizen, for out of his meeting with Kingsborough could come betrayal, and Kathleen's death.

"Faster, faster!" I cried, and Mia thundered along in the moonlight.

Fight at Dawn

South of Arklow I turned Mia east for the sea, calculating that the tide was out and I would make
quicker time by galloping along the strand. Hundreds
of refugees from Gorey were sleeping under the
hedges near the town, and I heard the wailing of
babies and the comforting sounds that come from
young mothers, but I heard no men. Later, I learned
that the Arklow commander was denying the people
entry, for he feared an uprising from within. Mia
lengthened her stride on the sands, and I knew that
if Hays had traveled inland he would make much
slower progress since the roads were packed with

wanderers. And I knew he hadn't taken to the strand, for there was no sign of hoofprints. I reckon Mia thought the mad woman of Gorey was still after her, for she'd be winning the Dublin Races the way she was traveling, and it was a fine night for galloping with the moon shimmering quicksilver on the sea. North of Arklow we came inland, and here I trotted Mia to a place where trees flocked over the road, and the poor soul was breathing like church bellows, for I had driven her fast.

"Rest yourself, girl," I said, and tethered her lightly. Then I climbed a tree that hung over the mud road and waited. With luck I was now ahead of Hays, and this was the only hope I had of stopping him from getting to Kingsborough.

Dawn was splitting the east with a chopper and red light was flooding over the world when I heard Hays coming. Up the hill he came, and I heard his big stallion snorting with the labor of it as they breasted a rise not a hundred yards away. Here Hays slowed to a trot and came toward me without a care in the world. The stallion reared and neighed in terror as I dropped from above, encircled Hays's body with my arms, and pulled him off, and we landed together in the dust with him underneath. He was momentarily stunned, and I managed to get a hand on the butt of his pistol. I drew it out, but immediately lost grip of it as Hays, recovering, snatched at my wrist. The pistol clattered away, and with a strength that astonished me, he threw me off and rose, drawing his rapier.

"You're a long way north of your maiden aunt in Waterford," he said.

I can see him now, magnificent in that strange red hue of dawn, the rapier a sliver of steel before him as he circled me, and I could see in a flash that he was an expert. Under the unwritten laws of chivalry I should have drawn, too, and fought it out, but he was doubtless a brilliant swordsman and I had far too much to lose. It was him or me, for the lives of Joe and Kathleen depended on me. Backing away, I drew my little pistol from the inside pocket of my doublet.

"Throw it down," I commanded, and approached him.

Momentarily he stared, then relaxed his big body and dropped the rapier. Taking a step forward, I stooped, snatched at it, and threw it away.

Lazily he put his fists on his hips and smiled.

"Well, shoot me and have done with it," he said.

I did not reply, and he added, "Or would you rather I turned so you could get me through the back?"

"You're not getting to Kingsborough, Hays," I said.

His horse was grazing nearer and nearer to us now

and I saw his eyes switch toward it. Mia also saw
the big stallion from her place deep in the woods,
and she neighed to him and he raised his fine brown
head and neighed reply.

Hays said quietly, "You realize you're makin' a
fool of yourself, I suppose. If I don't get to Kingsborough within the hour he'll not set sail for Wexford."

"If you get to Kingsborough he'll never set sail
at all," I replied. "You know as well as I do that he's
sailing into a trap."

"And that's exactly the intention, isn't it?"

"It's not yours, Hays."

"Would you believe me if I gave me solemn word
on it—that I'm working with the rebels?"

"If you are, then Caine Adams has no knowledge
of it," I answered. "According to him you've been
spying for the North Cork since the start of the rebellion, and probably before that."

Suddenly, to my astonishment, he dropped to his
knees and crossed himself, saying softly, "By the
holy God, I swear I'm acting for the rebels. In the
name of the Virgin I tell ye this, lad—I'm riding to
Kingsborough to tell him it's safe to sail on Wexford." He rose. "And if you don't believe me, then
shoot me an' have done wi' it, for I'm deep in misery
enough." Turning his back on me, he cried, "Shoot,

man, shoot, for I lost my all some three days back, and now I don't care if I live or die."

And fool that I was, I lowered the pistol in blank amazement, and in that split second of carelessness, Hays spun on his heel and dived at me, sending the pistol flying and bringing me down. Pinned beneath him I caught a glimpse of his face and it was filled with fury. He cried aloud as he brought down his fist, but I managed to block it and the blow struck me in the chest, the force of it pumping the breath from my body. I arched my back and threw him over, and we rose, fists clenched tight, gasping, circling each other.

I was standing between him and his horse, and he knew that I was waiting for him to come. He came on, hooking fiercely, but I stood my ground and prodded him off with a left. Blood trickled from his mouth, staining the lace collar of his shirt, but he only grinned and wiped it away with the back of his hand and came again, feet planted, swinging and hooking. I blocked one hook, rode another, but took the next right full but high. An inch lower and it would have been over. He came again as I retreated, teeth clenched, his bright fair hair falling over his brow, and I went back in a circle, prodding him away, each blow clear and clean and with the knuckles, but it was like hitting a brick wall. I caught him with swings, and one was full to the jaw, but it never even staggered him, and I think he knew that he had my measure. He was grinning, enjoying the fight while I was becoming desperate, for when it comes to a rough and tumble it is not only strength and size that count, it is also age. I might be younger and quicker, but this man was fully mature. And though I got in three blows to his one, nothing seemed to stop his onward plunge and swinging fists.

Suddenly he cried, "Of all the young idiots! Is this what they told you to do? Why didn't they keep ye safe in Wexford where you belong, and leave this business to grown men?" And he crouched and hooked me hard to the face in a sudden, bitter anger he had not shown before. Blow after blow was thudding into me now, and I began to gasp with pain as they sank deep into my body. Mistily, I saw Hays let fly with a vicious uppercut, but I did not feel the blow for my senses were numbed by the punishment. But I remember falling, and the dew was heavy on the grass, a healing balm to the thumps and pain of it all. The dawn exploded into violent light, and a great weight seemed suddenly to be released from my body. I floated in a world of darkness and peace.

When I returned to consciousness, Mia was standing above me, soft whinnies of misery coming from her throat. Slowly, I sat up, staring down the empty road. Hays had gone, taking my pistol and rapier. Doubtless, he had also tried to take Mia, but others had tried this in my father's time and failed. Now she watched with interest as I knelt beside the road and splashed cold water over my face and neck. Within a minute or two I rose and clambered into the saddle. The danger to Joe and Kathleen had returned to me with sickening force.

"Quick, quick!" I whispered. "Away, girl—on to Mizen!"

And Mia, refreshed by the rest, lengthened her stride and took us over the fields at a rare speed.

"On, on, girl!" I cried.

Rounding a heading of land I saw a lonely fishing smack lazing in a little inlet, and I knew by instinct that this was the boat of Joe Lehane. Just off the road was a little farm, and I reined Mia into its stackyard, crying, "Anyone home?"

Almost at once a window opened and a grizzled old head came out, and under it was a fowling piece. A voice cried, "Who the devil is creatin' all this palaver at such a time in the mornin'?"

"Stabling for the mare, until I come back for her!" I shouted back, watching the fowling piece, for there was a habit in Ireland now of shooting first and questioning afterward.

"Are ye loyalist or rebel, son?"

Taking a chance, I shouted, "Rebel, same as all decent Irishmen. And Wexfree's the password."

"That's it!" came the answer. "You're in the right house. For had ye been North Cork or Armagh Militia I'd have blown ye to blazes. Tether the horse and leave it, son, for we had a stripling like you two months back, God rest him."

I stood decent for him.

"What's your name, boy?"

"John Regan."

"Right, now away and let us sleep. And if ever the rebels need a service round these parts they need look no farther than Maude and Ahab Dickie."

I did not delay, but hitched Mia outside his door and ran. For if Joe Lehane was needing help I could give it better without a horse hanging round my neck. I ran first along the fields and then down to the strand, and the sand was sailing up behind me and falling in lazy thumps as I went. I skidded round a promontory. The boat was in sight now; she was coming slowly toward the shore. But I saw something more important. Above her sails, unseen by Joe or Kathleen, a troop of horsemen were trotting along the edge of the sea, making their way down to the tiny jetty.

Kathleen rose in the stern, gripped the tiller and

waved frantically as I floundered in the shallows toward the boat.

"John Regan!" she exclaimed as I hauled myself over the gunwale. "Who's been chopping firewood on your face?"

"No odds to that," I shouted. "Where's your father?"

Joe Lehane came scrambling up from the cabin at the commotion.

"Patrick Hays, the informer, has got through to Mizen, and we'll have to keep watch for a North Cork troop, for I've heard there's one coming!" I cried.

"Have ye now!" said he, eyeing me up and down. "And what kind of warning do ye call this, then?"

"I came the moment I could, sir," I said.

"Did ye? Well, it's not soon enough. There's four horsemen coming down from the Head right now, and I'm praying to God that it's Kingsborough. Because if it's not, it'll be the North Cork coming to arrest us. They'll be here in five minutes—do you call that a warning?" Joe spat in disgust. "They've got cannon on this water that'll blow us out of the bay if I shift us now."

"Oh, for the love of God!" whispered Kathleen, her hands to her face.

"Aye, and what else can I do, woman, but stay

and take the chance?" cried Joe, swinging back to me. "Was Father John in Wexford at the time Hays and you left?"

"No, sir," I replied.

"And did Hays know the rebels were marching on the town?"

"He agreed with me that Father John would probably march on Newtownbarry, to open the road to Wicklow and the north. But I reckon he knows the truth of it—that they're marching on Wexford this minute."

Joe stared at me then, changing the subject. "Your face is in a whale of a state—how did it get like that?"

"I tried to stop Hays," I said.

He put his hands on his hips. "You did, eh? And did Caine Adams instruct you to tamper with the man?" His voice rose. "Didn't Caine Adams tell you you'd be responsible to the Wexford rebels if you delayed the fella or harmed a hair of his head?"

"He did, sir."

"Then why, in heaven's name, did ye do it?"

"I met with some rebels at Ballymoney," I explained, "and they told me the North Cork have been checking on you. An informer betrayed you and I reckoned that Hays knew the truth of you, too, and Kingsborough would arrest you on his evidence."

"And so ye tried to stop Hays, is it, to save us?"

I nodded, and he said, screwing up his face, "Marvelous. Father John is going to be delighted wi' you." His voice rose. "Will ye tell me the worth of military orders if they're not going to be obeyed?"

"Och!" exclaimed Kathleen. "He only did it for us."

"You get below," commanded Joe. Tense, we listened. Above the slapping of water came the sound of voices and laughter. "It's Kingsborough, thank God," whispered Joe. "Get you into the anchor locker. Kath will find ye a brace of pistols and tell ye what to do. If they take us prisoner, raise the rebels around here and get word to Father John and Adams as quick as you can—"

"We could fight for it!"

Joe said, "We're not fighting. If Kingsborough comes to harm, the rebels themselves would string us up. It's a live hostage Father John's after, not a dead colonel. Away! If there's something queer goin' on and we still sail for Wexford, come out of the locker and cover them while I take care of Hays up on deck. Quick now!"

I went down the tiny companionway and into a little cabin with a chart table. Up forward I found the door of the anchor locker and crept inside, and I was about to shut it when Kathleen crawled up on her hands and knees.

"When I drop a bottle in the cabin, it's your signal

to come out and cover all three officers—me father will cover Hays by the wheel while I disarm Kingsborough and the other two." She handed me a pair of long-barreled pistols.

"All three of them, eh?"

"You just cover 'em and I'll disarm them," said she, "three or three hundred."

I said, "Let me know when you want a fella to walk out with, Kath," and in the moment before she shut the locker door she fluttered me an Irish wink. "Och, the chance'd be a fine thing—you with a black eye an' your nose all over your face!"

When the kissing is stopped you've still got the cooking, so the saying goes; but give me pluck at a time like this. I'm hanging up me hat in that one's parlor, I thought, although she doesn't know it.

The Hostage

Within five minutes the four of them came aboard the smack, and were large as life and twice as boisterous, with only one object in mind—a sail down to Wexford town through St. George's Channel. Peering through a crack in my locker, I watched them trooping into the chartroom. And although I couldn't hear a word that was said, one thing was sure: Hays was pretty well in with them, for Lord Kingsborough had his hand on his shoulder, talking like brother to brother. Earlier too I had heard them searching the boat, poking here and there in the chartroom while I watched them, my body tense. The big Hompesch German started tapping with his knuckles around the bunk cupboard. Immediately, Joe came over to the locker door and tapped it within an inch of my nose.

"Anchor ropes," he said. "I opened this when I came aboard."

The German grunted and rose, moving to the chart table. He was a handful, this one, and I examined my pistols closer. Then, above a whistle of the wind I heard Joe's hoarse shouts to Kathleen to cast off stern and prow, and the little boat collected the wind and heeled, and the prow made a thunder as we cut for mid-channel.

Sitting there in the darkness I began to wonder what Hays was up to, and decided to try to take him first, if I could. And if I killed him doing it, it would be no loss to Ireland. A known informer and spy for the hated North Cork, he had done more damage to the rebel cause than a hundred loyalist soldiers. And it might just as well be that he knew Wexford would be free of rebels, and was taking Joe and Kathleen into a trap that would end on a rope. I clenched shut my eyes in that darkness and prayed as never before. I would rather have died at his hands outside Arklow than see Kathleen at the mercy of the North Cork Militia.

By the time midday came I was cramped as a

mummy in that anchor locker, for the only time I dared to take a bit of a stretch was when Lord Kingsborough and the rest were strolling up on deck. I could hear the stamp of their feet above me as they hung onto things, for the smack began bucking and leaping like a live thing the moment we struck the Curracloe currents.

And then, about one o'clock, I heard a cultured voice cry above the howling wind, "Curracloe coming up, Lehane! Keep her over to larboard so we can see if the harbor is clear!"

It was the voice of Lord Kingsborough.

"Keeping her larboard, sir," came Joe's stifled reply.

"Lay over still more, Lehane!" I instantly recognized this voice as Hays's. The smack heeled again, then righted, running goosewinged and free before the northeasterly.

"Keep her on that!" shouted Hays.

"Aye, aye," cried Joe, and I crouched in a strange, uncanny silence since we were no longer on the tack but wallowing in long leaps for the distant channel off Wexford Bay. The sun beat down on the roof of the locker and the air within was stifling. Sweat ran in streams down my face and neck, and I lay back on a rope coil with the pistols on the floor beside me, tuning my ears to every sound. A board creaked in the chartroom beyond, and I put my eye to the crack, peering into the room.

Hays was standing alone at the chart table. He was swiftly priming a pair of pistols. And the moment he had thrust them into his belt, Lord Kingsborough and the two officers appeared on the companionway. We must have been nearing the mouth of the harbor because all three began buckling on their sword belts and talking good-humoredly.

Then Joe's face appeared in the doorway. "Shall I take her in, sir?"

"Yes, take us in, Lehane," called Kingsborough, and at that moment Kathleen came down into the cabin carrying a tray of glasses and a bottle.

"Mr. Hays," called Joe Lehane then, "will ye come up on deck a minute?"

Hays went up and the door closed behind him. With Kathleen and the three officers alone in the cabin, I crouched, one foot against the locker door, waiting for her signal.

Suddenly I heard the whistle of a shot, and a crash in the sea. The ketch shuddered from prow to stern and began to heel. Way over she heeled, and I thought she was never coming back. Distantly, from the sea, came the dull boom of cannon, and I realized that we were being fired upon. Again a boom, and a soft, high-pitched whistling that ended in a scream as the big ball whistled overhead. Then a wall of water struck the smack; the flow from the first shot had sent up a plume of sea on the larboard bow. The impact bowled me over and I snatched at the two pistols on the floor, but too late, for the floor was swilling in water as the seams parted at the prow, and the sea was spurting in, drenching me. The pistols were useless, for the priming was soaked.

Faintly then I heard Kingsborough's voice. "Go about, Lehane! Go about!"

One of the escort officers leaped up the companionway. I heard him stamping on the deck above, and then his thin cry, "It's the oyster boats, your lordship! They're firing from the oyster boats!" He came down into the cabin, drenched and breathless, and said to Kingsborough, "It's mounted shore-cannon, too, sir—the place must be rebel held!"

"Don't be a fool, man!"

"I tell you I saw them through the glass, sir. The town is packed with rebels. All down the Common Quay they're fluttering the rebel green!"

And at that moment Kathleen dropped her tray in a sudden crash of glass. The door of the anchor locker flew open as I kicked with both feet and crawled out into the chartroom, both pistols leveled. Never will I forget the utter astonishment on Kingsborough's face. And the two escorts also stared in disbelief. Kingsborough was the first to recover himself.

"Who the devil are you?" he breathed as he backed away.

I said, "Just do as you're told, man, and no harm'll befall you." I braced my feet against the bulwarks and the three officers gripped the chart table, for the ketch was still rolling madly.

Kingsborough said, "I remember you. You're the North Cork who brought the message from headquarters—" He was staring at me over his shoulder.

"Not a move," I said. "One move, and it'll be your last. Are you there, Kathleen?"

"Aye, here!"

"Quick," I whispered, "before Hays comes back."

As Kathleen disarmed him Kingsborough said, "Now I remember that face and that voice. They belong to Sean Regan, the United Irishman of Milford."

"My father," I replied, taking the pistols from Kathleen and tossing them into the locker. "And he died for a free and decent Ireland, for all the things you hate."

"Like you will die before this rebellion is over, Regan."

"Perhaps," I said, "but now we'll have your life to bargain with, and we'll use it well. See to Captain

Bourke next, Kathleen. His fingers are itching for his sword, and I don't trust him."

She nodded, running round the escort German, and as she did so Bourke, moving with the speed of the trained soldier, snatched her wrist and drew her body across his as a shield. As I leaped to help her, Kingsborough darted for the locker and his pistol.

"Hays, Hays!" It was Kingsborough shouting as I lurched after him, kicking shut the locker door, and the second I turned the German escort was upon me, dragging me down.

"Right, that is enough," said Kingsborough, and he leveled Bourke's pistol.

Stupidly, I stood there with the soaked pistols drooping in my hands.

"Drop those," said Kingsborough, and I did so. Then he looked at the companionway and shouted, "Hays, Hays! Where the devil are you, man?"

I stared past Kingsborough at the door. Hays was standing there, and his two long-barreled pistols were trained on Lord Kingsborough's back.

"Yes, and you drop yours, too," said Hays. "No, don't turn, sir—or I'll blow your soul to kingdom come. I said drop it!"

The little pistol fell at Kingsborough's feet. "Are you mad, Hays?"

"Well done," said Hays. "And the first man who

stirs gets a barrel." He jerked his head. "Kathleen—upstairs on deck and help your father. Signal those rebel oyster boats, or they'll blow us out of the water. You, lad," and he motioned a pistol at me. "There's rope in plenty in that anchor locker. Fetch some out."

"There's no need for rope," said Lord Kingsborough. "The guns have the better of us." He was still staring in disbelief at Hays.

"That may be so, your lordship," replied Hays coolly, "but I'm inclined to distrust your bodyguard." Leaning forward he drew the adjutant's sword and tossed it into a corner; taking his pistol, too, he thrust it into his own belt. "Tie them well, lad, for your life may depend on it—you gave me an outing indeed last night and I'm short-tempered wi' you." He gave me a grin, but I didn't return it. I was still dazed from the struggle and the sight of him standing there, one moment a loyalist, the next a rebel.

As I was tying the officers' wrists, Lord Kingsborough said, "I'd have trusted my life to you, Hays —indeed, I did today. What's happened to you, man? For years you've been a loyal soldier and a true friend of the North Cork."

"You've looked no farther than your nose, your lordship," replied Hays, smiling, "if you really believe that!"

"The man's been a damned traitor all the time—that's my guess," said Captain Bourke, the adjutant.

"It is a pity you did not guess it before, Captain!" said the Hompesch.

Kingsborough said, "Is that true, Hays?"

Patrick Hays replied slowly, "Had I been the dirty loyalist you took me for, Kingsborough, then God forgive me, for me prayer is for an independent Ireland, free from the clutches of the likes of you. But had I been such a traitorous lackey, I'd have changed me tune a couple of days back when you murdered my son up on Killthomas, so you'd still have landed here."

The Hompesch said, "We kill your son? It was not the North Cork or the Hessians. It was Gorey yeomen who cut them to pieces up on Killthomas."

"I'm not splittin' hairs on it, German," said Hays. "An eye for an eye, that is what the Good Book says, and I'm obeying it." He straightened before them. "My lad died fighting against the things you stand for, and he was wearing the rebel green. Any father in his right senses would change to the same color, for the tunic of his enemies is the color of blood."

"May God forgive you, Hays," said Kingsborough, as Joe Lehane and I prodded him up on deck. "And you, too, Lehane—we'll show you no mercy when our time comes, remember."

"When it comes," replied Joe, prodding with a pistol. "Meanwhile may God forgive you and your kind for the unholy state of Ireland."

Turncoat

Golden light was flashing on the sea as Joe took the fishing smack alongside the Common Quay of Wexford, escorted by the oyster boats, which had done fine work in the sea patrols, bringing in ships bound for Dublin loaded with provisions. So there was no shortage of food in gay rebel Wexford, with the people happy and well fed and every man jack of them wearing the green. Green was everywhere, hanging from the windows of the fishermen's cottages, in the hair of the women. Great boughs of it decorated the masts of ships in the harbor, waving in wands from the musket barrels of the guard that awaited the coming of Lord Kingsborough and his officers. Captain Matthew Keugh, now the rebel governor of Wexford, looked resplendent in his bright green uniform, and he saluted Lord Kingsborough as he came down the gangplank and the rebel soldiers formed up about him.

Great was the rejoicing as Kingsborough was taken off to the prison ship, with fiddlers playing and tambourines rattling from the gypsies. Street urchins who had not seen a bath since the midwife, danced together in fairy rings. Kathleen and I leaned on the rail of the smack and watched it all, and there was in me a great peace that we had unloaded Kingsborough ashore, and that Kathleen was unharmed, though quite naturally I didn't make too much of it.

"Will ye be coming back to Enniscorthy now the war is over?" she asked, and there was a great beauty in her standing there with the sun on her and green ribbons hanging in her hair.

I shrugged. "I might—when the war is over, and it isn't over yet."

"But you'll come as a decent working fella, in Enniscorthy, when the peace of Ireland is won?"

"I might," I said, "though I'm partial to Milford, ye know, where me mother came from."

"Och, 'tis Wales that, not Ireland! What would ye be wanting with a heathen place like Milford?"

I emptied my hands at her. "I'll give it some thought, but one place is as good as another."

"Och, aye!" said she, her eyes glowing. "And there's better fish in the sea than ever came out o' it."

Mind, it would take a regiment of Hessians to keep me out of Enniscorthy once Kathleen Lehane was going back to it, but it's a fatal thing to let the woman in on a chap's intentions.

I was just on the point of leading her on a bit more when someone called from the stern rail, and I turned and saw Hays standing there alone.

"Can ye bide here a moment, Regan?" said he.

I went to him, and he said, smiling, "You're a big boy, son, and wi' a bit more flesh on your bones you'll be a handful for any man." He grinned, rubbing his jaw. "Indeed, ye caused me more trouble than I expected, for all the gangling youth of ye. How old you be?"

"Seventeen."

He turned from me, looking at the quay where the folk were dancing in a bright medley of waving scarves and skirts and celebration muskets were spitting fire and booms. His eyes were narrowed against the sun and I suspected in them a hint of tears. He said, "It hurt me sore to be handing it out to ye outside Arklow, for you're the spit o' the son I hoped mine to be, all skin and bone and wi' your hair bright gold, the same as he." He turned on the rail. "You hear they killed him up on Killthomas?"

"Aye," I whispered, and a little wind blew between us, as a balm.

Hays said, "D'you see this wee thing?" He fished in his pocket and brought out a locket with a broken chain, and I stared at it. It was the locket the dying boy had given me up on the hill above Ennis. Hays continued, "It was handed to Father John Murphy by a chap who was with my boy when he died, and my lad asked that it be given to my wife. But Father John reckoned I should have it first, seeing my name and address are in it." He sighed deep. "It's a queer, sad life when you come to think of it."

"Yes."

Hays said, "And Father John wrote me a letter with it, telling how my lad had fought with Father Patrick and Father Sweeney—and they died, too, he said, up on Killthomas." He opened the locket and held in his fingers a tiny lock of hair. "Queer, isn't it, that he should have been wearing that round his neck when he died. It was a gift to his mother, so he must have got it from her box."

"How did you get that locket, then?" I asked.

"The landlord of the Parrot handed it to me in Wexford, though I didn't open the packet till after I'd left him, so how he came by it I don't know." He ran his fingers through his bright hair and looked at me. "I don't know how he came by it, though I've got my suspicions, but I'd give my life to meet the man who was with my boy when he died up on Killthomas."

Just then Kathleen called, "John Regan, are ye coming? I've been waiting these past minutes— they're dancing in the streets along the road to Ennis!"

"Just give me a couple of minutes," I called back.

To Patrick Hays I said softly, "It was me, sir—it was me with him. And I reckon I delivered that locket to the Parrot landlord without knowing it. Your son went easy, as easy as a sigh, with the bells of Enniscorthy calling for mass, and there was a light in him and your name was on his lips, and he told me you were fighting for the rebel cause and Father John Murphy and the things he believes in."

"It was you, then. I guessed it, son. Dear God, I couldn't have laid a rough finger on you outside Arklow had I known it was you. My son had the truth of me—d'you realize that? He was the only soul in the world save the leaders who had the truth of me." I stared at him, but he turned away.

Now there was a lot of pushing and shoving below, for Captain Keugh, the governor of Wexford, was shouting, "Will someone take me to the lad who tricked Lord Kingsborough into coming, for Father John Murphy is after giving him personal congratulations."

I said to Joe, "It's Patrick Hays here who managed it. I got the size of myself sir, when you put me up against a professional."

Hays said, "Have ye got a bit of rebel green I could tie round me neck, Regan?"

He looked the image of his dead son standing there as I took off my scarf and ripped it down the middle and tossed him half. Turning away, he knotted it on.

"Patrick Hays," said Joe Lehane, "Father John himself is asking for you, and you're to report this instant, or it'll be sore with ye."

"Aye, indeed," returned Hays, grimly, "they make their rebel ropes wi' hemp just the same as they do in the loyalist militia."

"I canna speak for Father John," Joe answered, "but you'll oblige me by taking off that rebel scarf before ye stand in front of him."

I said, as Patrick Hays removed the scarf, "Is this the way you reward a service? Do you realize that Kingsborough would still be back in Mizen Head if it wasn't for Patrick Hays here?"

Joe replied, "And do you realize that ye can't wipe out years of betrayal by a single act of turning your coat? This fella's a wanted man, and he'll get the treatment he deserves from better brains than yours, so stand aside, lad."

The crowd was thicker on the quay now. The little fat landlord of the Parrot stood in the foreground, and he cried, his fist up, "Me son-in-law was hanged on the foul creature's testimony! Not two months back he was hanged in the Dublin gaol side by side with wee Sean Dickie, the son of Maude and Ahab! Do ye deny it, Patrick Hays?"

Another shouted, "He turned his coat to save his skin—can't ye see the size of it? I say hang him here and 'ave done with it, for he deserves nothing less!" In growing horror, I knew Hays for what he was—informer.

Even the sun froze. The cold hand of death began to move along the quay, and the crowd pressed closer, their rebel faces inflamed with passion. And from their ranks came a man called Dixon, later to be known as Bloody Dixon for the atrocities he committed on Wexford Bridge, and he cried aloud, "I say take him, men. Are there any good patriots here?"

"Aye, aye!" A forest of hands and pikes were raised high in a tumultuous cheer.

"I say take him and have done wi' him in the holy name of Ireland. The pitch cap first, and then a hanging! And we will show all traitor Irish, yeomen or militia loyalists, that they cannot trifle with the people. Come, take him!"

The bodyguard of the rebel governor was breaking through to us, and they forced the crowd back with crossed pikes and curses. I chanced a look at Patrick Hays. He was staring at the sea, oblivious to the clamor about him, the cries for his blood, and I knew what he was thinking. He was no longer on the quay at Wexford; he was up on Killthomas Hill with his son. And his lips moved even as I watched him.

"My sweet, wee Jeff," he said.

I turned away as the guard led him down into Wexford town, under rebel escort, to appear before Father John Murphy.

The Twist in the Tale

I managed to get away from the quay with Kathleen before the rebel governor arrived, for if there's anything that frightens me it is heartiest congratulations, especially in this case, for they belonged to Patrick Hays.

For all the allegations of his crimes, for all the accusations the rebels flung in his face, it seemed to me that a great light shone from him. And it also struck me as queer that his dying son's last words were for the love of him, for there can't be a whole lot wrong with a man who's idolized by his son.

"Come on, come on!" cried Kathleen, her hair flying.

And she caught my hand and we were into the dancing, for the rebels had declared it a public holiday in Wexford now that Kingsborough was under lock and key. The dancing was in full swing, with flutes and fiddles and melodeons going and muskets popping and the shore cannon booming, with everybody in the gayest colors kicking up their legs on the cobbles.

But I could not dance, for the face of Patrick Hays was moving before me. I knew that if vicious rebels like Dixon had their way he'd be swinging from the nearest bracket before midday.

"What ails ye, Regan?" demanded Kathleen, all flushed and beautiful. "You've a face as long as a kite. Are ye dancing or not?"

"I'm thinking about Patrick Hays," I answered.

"And would he be thinking about you? The man's a loyalist spy—cease wasting your time on the likes of him when there's dancing to be had!"

She gripped my waist and began to swing me around to the beat of the music, and there was nought to do but give her her way.

Just then a fellow came to the edge of the crowd and yelled, "Is John Regan of Milford in there?"

"Och, forget him!" cried Kathleen, pulling me on, her hair flying.

"He is!" I yelled back. "What do you want with him?"

"Then come out this minute, for you're summoned before the committee!"

I pulled myself out of the crowd and Kathleen was stamping her foot, her fist up at me. "I'll find meself another chap, remember!" she cried.

I got to the man. "What committee?" I asked him.

"The United Irishmen, and it's sitting under the hand of Bagenal Harvey, so you'd best make it sharp."

"What does Bagenal Harvey want with the likes of me?" I gasped.

"One thing's sure, man—it's either death or glory. Follow me."

The committee was sitting in a little courthouse behind the gaol, and my heart was thudding against my shirt as I stood outside the door, brushing the dust off me and smoothing down my hair, for it's a fearful thing to be called before a committee of the United Irishmen. I remember my father telling me with pride that it nearly happened to him, and he couldn't sleep for days before, such was the importance of it.

Outside the window the rebels were parading, for squads of them had been issued with muskets from Camolin. And faintly I could hear the hammering of the carpenters on Wexford Bridge, making a gallows. There were some loyalist criminals in town that day who would never see the sun set because of their crimes against the people. Kingsborough himself might be one of those to be tried, so there was little hope for the likes of Patrick Hays, the North Cork spy, I thought.

"John Regan!" A voice came faintly from within the room, and I recognized it instantly, the beloved bass of Father John Murphy.

The door of the courtroom swung open and a guard appeared.

Slowly I entered, my breath pent. And before me, at a half circle of tables, sat the men of destiny, the heroes of the rebel cause. No less than fifteen men sat there, their eyes fixed on my face. Bagenal Harvey was in the middle, his gaze piercing with the quality of steel. Beside him was Captain Keugh, the rebel governor, and on the other side Cornelius Grogan, the aged rebel landowner of whom I had heard. I saw John Colclough, young and handsome, and Father Roche, the giant priest who fought at the battle of Three Rocks. And also his friend, Father Bush, who once, under the torture of the whips, said, "Do not cease; my Saviour has suffered more than this." Edward Roche was also there with his brother —Edward who had deserted with a thousand Catholic troops and joined the rebel cause because of the inhumanity of the loyalists. Others, many others, were there, their names a legend in Ireland already. And among them was Father John Murphy. He did a little smile at me, his eyes twinkling.

"Come in, son, nobody's going to eat ye," he said.

I approached and stood at attention before Bagenal Harvey. The room echoed in extraordinary, tomblike silence, and I heard the beating of my heart.

"Your name is John Regan?" Bagenal Harvey glanced up at me.

"Yes, sir."

"The son of Sean Regan, the United Irishman of Milford?"

I did not reply, but straightened before him. He said softly, "My congratulations, Regan, on possessing such a father. He was a man who obeyed military instructions to the letter. Why do you not obey them?"

I clenched my hands and lowered my eyes from his.

The leader said, "You have taken the oath of the United Irishmen?"

"Yes, sir."

"And sworn to obey the Cause?"

I nodded, and he said, "Then why do you not do so? You were given specific instructions by Caine Adams in Enniscorthy. You were ordered to track Patrick Hays on his way north from Wexford, and inform Lehane and his daughter whether he had gone to the Mizen camp or not. You chose, instead, to take the law into your own hands—to attack and delay him. Why did you do this?"

"Because he was an enemy of the people, sir."

"Yet he managed to persuade Lord Kingsborough and two North Cork officers to enter rebel-occupied Wexford? How do you account for that?"

It was as if my life was balanced on a needle-point of pain. I did not care what they did to me—for my life, compared to the Cause, was not important. It was the disgrace of it, being shamed before the memory of my father.

Bagenal Harvey said, "Now you see the foolishness of not obeying orders to the letter. Would your father have behaved like this? Did you know, for instance, that you were being used as bait—somebody to be trapped and shot at by rebel and loyalist alike, while the real messenger got through to trap Kingsborough?"

A voice behind me said, "He's a serious youngster, Colonel. He hit me so hard that I gave up hope of trapping anybody!"

I swung round on my heel. Patrick Hays was standing against the wall at the door, his hands behind his back, and he was smiling. And he was dressed fine from head to foot in rebel green, in the uniform of a captain of infantry. Coming forward, he said, "But if the Ballymoney rebels had got me instead of Regan here, I reckon I'd still be swinging. And he caught me a couple of right hooks north of Arklow that had me shoutin' for me mother. In fact, sir," he said to the committee, "if I ask to be backed by a second string again I'm doing my own choosing, an' it'll be one a sight less keen than this one here, for I nearly didn't get to Mizen Head and Kingsborough."

I stared at them. Others were speaking now; laughter at my discomfiture was rising round the room, and I could do nothing more than stare. It was the incredible efficiency of them, the astonishing planning that dumbfounded me. And I realized then that I had been selected as the bait for any possible attack on Patrick Hays, that they dared not tell me this lest I had been captured and talked under torture. I realized, too, that he was a double agent, one who for years had been in the pay of Kingsborough's North Cork Militia, while working secretly for the United Irishmen.

Bagenal Harvey said then, "You have a right to be surprised, Regan—even angered—but remember this. We are not concerned with your emotions, only with your loyalty and skill. And you have proved that you possess the first in great measure. A cooler head will temper the second quality, and this you will learn, too, because you are still young." His eyes softened momentarily, and he looked at Father John. "Father Murphy thought you too young for the job with Hays, and the committee gives its congratulations to Joseph Lehane and Caine Adams, both of whom recommended you. The committee of United Irishmen also thanks you for your service, and recommends that you accompany Patrick Hays on a mission to France. But wait!" His hand went up.

An unbounded joy was rising within me. I closed my eyes to a surge of unforgivable pride—that I, John Regan, should be given the chance of following in the footsteps of my famous father. And when I opened them, Father John Murphy had risen to his feet and his face was grave.

He said in a deep voice, "Know this, John Regan. The decision is yours, but do not make it lightly. The mission of Patrick Hays to France is accompanied by the gravest danger. It is necessary for us to join with Wolfe Tone, the Irish patriot, in the service of Napoleon Bonaparte in his efforts to raise a French invasion force which will fight side by side with us to free the land. The enemies of the rebellion are about us on all sides; spies and counter-spies have already been sent from London, men who will stop at nothing. Think on this. The odds of either you or

Patrick Hays coming out of this alive are loaded against you."

Silence fell over the room, as if the hand of death had entered. Then I heard myself say, "What—what are the odds, Holy Father?"

"Caine Adams reckons them at ten to one."

The wind whispered in the eaves of the building, and Caine Adams rose and said softly, "These are favorable odds, young Regan. The man who accepts them must assume that once he leaves this land, he will not return to it. The rope, the galleys, who knows?"

I swallowed hard, dry in my throat. All eyes were upon me. Suddenly I had a flash vision of my father's face, square and strong. He too, I recalled with mounting pride, had been sent on a mission to Bonaparte in support of the great Irishman, Theobald Wolfe Tone. But the galleys! The terrible corsairs! Death might be acceptable, but the thought of the chained labor of the oars, the lash of the overseer's whip, had never failed to terrify me.

Bagenal Harvey said now, "Take your time, lad, for you have a long life before you. And remember, too, that if you accept this proposition, you lose every friend in the world—as Patrick Hays has lost his in the cause of secrecy. You'll be cursed by decent Irish, an outcast, the dirt on any man's tongue. Aye, take your time." He added, "And don't forget the odds against returning."

I turned to Patrick Hays. He was smiling, and I saw in that smile the face of Jeff, his son. I asked, "Do you accept these odds, sir?"

He drew himself up. "For God, for honor, for Ireland," he said, and bowed deep to me. I turned back to the committee.

"Aye," I said. "The pair of us—him and me. For God, for honor, for the beloved country."

Bagenal Harvey nodded. "The privilege is yours, not Ireland's—this is what she expects of you. Our lives are worthless compared to her glory. Usher, bring in the next, please—the hostages of Wexford: Kingsborough, Bourke, and the Hompesch soldier. Good luck, Hays and Regan, may God be good to ye."

Kathleen was awaiting me outside the courthouse, and she was in a terrible dither, dabbing at her eyes with a little lace handkerchief, and why didn't ye tell me you were appearing before the Rebel Committee, for I've been worried sick to death for ye.

Old Joe slipped a wink at me.

"Och, it was nothing," I said, smiling at Joe. "They were only after evidence for the trial of Patrick Hays, the North Cork spy."

"Is it true they're hanging him at midday on the bridge?"

"Already hung," I said. "They had him on a rope's end five minutes after I gave my evidence, and good riddance." I gave Joe a wink and whispered, "I'll never forgive ye. You knew all the time."

"Poor soul," said Kathleen. "He had a fine face and a goodly air about him. Do ye think he'd mind, John Regan, if we went back to the dancing for a little minute?"

"Well, now, girl—" I took her hand.

"Do you mean to say you're not coming, and I've been waitin' here all the morning!"

"It's like this, you see," I whispered. "I've a spot of business to attend to, but I'll get free from it the moment I can . . ."

"You rapscallion!" cried she. "You've got me dancing on the end of a string. If ye'll not come for the music and gaiety I'll soon find another fella who will." She smacked my hands away. "Is rebellion and fighting all ye ever think of? Oh, John, is it heart to heart the pair of us and never hand to hand? Will ye come, just this once? Listen, man, *listen!* It's the Irish fiddlers playing, and the flutes of Donegal, and the gypsies are singing. Oh, come, come!"

"Good-by," I said. A short, sharp pain is best with good-bys.

I looked back once. Joe had his arms about her and her hands were over her face. I pitied her, knowing a strange emptiness, for there was within me a yearning for her that had no place in my fight for my beloved Ireland.

I pushed the dancers aside and took the road out of Wexford town, the road that led to Mizen Head and the farm of Maude and Ahab Dickie, who were stabling Mia until I should return.

After that I would ride to Wicklow, as Patrick Hays had instructed me, and meet him in secret at midnight in two days' time, in the shadow of the Old Mill in the Tangles of Maro. And there, it was agreed, a little ketch would be waiting one day; a little ketch with the cutthroat sails of Corsica, which would carry us both to France.

I grinned as I walked those Irish lanes, for the sun was burning hot with the heat of midday and the beloved country was all dressed up in her Sunday best of rebel green, and the sky was a varnished blue, with bed-sheet clouds blowing over the rim of the world. And then I remembered Mia, and gave a secret grin. I might have lost an Irish maid but Mia, at least, was heading for romance. She had shown a mad rolling eye for Patrick Hays's big brown horse last time they met.

And, remembering this, I was a wee bit jealous.

Strange, I reflected, that Mia was the only real friend I had ever known, save Joe and Kathleen.

Laughing at the sky, I broke into a gentle, swaying run, snatching at the tree buds as I passed. After a bit I rested beneath a tree, watching a lark nicking and diving over the gorgeous, rolling land. Here I knelt, thinking of the little rebel I had met on the road outside Naas, the little five-foot soldier who was for stopping the advance of the Armagh Militia alone.

Thinking of him, I remembered what he did when I left him. And in memory of him, I copied his act of worship and dug my fingers deep into the soil of my country and held it before my face.

"If they're sending me to the foreign places after the battle for Wexford, then you're coming too," I said, and I put the soil of Ireland into my pocket.

Now for two days of leave, two days of wandering my own, sweet land. Come what may, I thought; come the whip and screw, the hangman's cord, the sweating oar of the Spanish galley or the stake itself, none could take from me this great, unbounded love.

In a quiet place of bushes, away from eyes, I prayed, which was the habit of my father. After this, I rose.

Head up and whistling to have my teeth out, I went cocky up that Irish lane on my way to fetch Mia. Boots thrusting out, puffing an Irish air, I went, and the sweet woman who was my country beat about me in all her perfume, and with a rare, green radiance.

With the knowledge that soon again I'd be in service to her, I went without a care.

:

Historical Characters in
Witches' Sabbath

LORD EDWARD FITZGERALD   Younger brother of the Duke of
Leinster. Once a member of the Irish Parliament, he served
in the American Revolution and was later dismissed from
the British Army because of his radical views. Distinguished
for his fine character and extreme good looks and for
his courage as a soldier, Lord Edward became one of the
early leaders of the United Irishmen, a society pledged to
free Ireland from British rule. This secret society was
formed in Belfast in 1791 by a young lawyer, Theobald
Wolfe Tone, and his friend Samuel Neilson.

   While Wolfe Tone was trying to raise another French
expedition to support an Irish rebellion against the British,
the 1798 rebellion broke out, and it was organized and led
by Lord Edward. However, the British government, with
spies everywhere, knew in advance of the rebels' plans,

and struck first. Most of the leaders of the United Irishmen in Ireland were arrested, and among the first to be captured was Lord Edward. He fought bitterly to resist arrest, was mortally wounded, and died some three weeks later. His courage and devotion to his country were above suspicion, his ideals lofty and unselfish. He died for what he considered a sacred cause.

BAGENAL HARVEY A Protestant landowner and a man of humane and kindly disposition. Bagenal Harvey was the owner of Bargy Castle at the time of the 1798 rebellion. Though possessed of great personal courage (he fought several duels), he was not a born leader, and it is thought that he took the leadership because of popular clamor rather than for any personal ambitions. He led the rebels in a violent attack on the town of New Ross on June 5, 1798, and at first it appeared certain that they were victorious. But General Johnson, the loyalist commander, counterattacked while the rebels were celebrating and drove them from the town. When the rebellion was eventually crushed, Bagenal Harvey, who for so long had striven for moderation and had done all in his power to prevent unnecessary bloodshed, was hanged with other conspirators on the old Wexford Bridge.

CAPTAIN MATTHEW KEUGH Cousin to Jonah Barrington and rebel governor of Wexford at the time of Bagenal Harvey's leadership. A man of great size, good looks and magnetic personality. Keugh did much to prevent rebel excesses and was spoken for by the influential Lord Kingsborough, commander of the infamous North Cork Militia. Like the other rebels, he too was hanged on Wexford Bridge. It is said that even in death his good looks did not desert him: that in the horrible exhibition of speared heads, his face maintained the same beauty and quiet resolution that had dignified it in life.

GENERAL GERARD LAKE   The General Officer commanding
the British and Irish loyalist forces at the time of the 1798
rebellion. A born soldier, he was inflexible in purpose and
merciless in victory. The sixty-five prominent persons
hanged on Wexford Bridge were but a small proportion of
the vast numbers who died at his command in revenge for
the rebellion. Even persons found unarmed in their own
houses were slain in cold blood. It is said that after he left
Ireland the women and children fled from the sight of a
British uniform as from an evil spirit.

FATHER JOHN MURPHY   This Catholic priest raised the first
standard of revolution at Boolavogue, a hamlet on the road
between Wexford and Gorey, on May 26, 1798. A statue to
Father John can be seen today in the square of Enniscorthy.
He is described by one set of historians as ignorant—a
narrow-minded fanatic; by others he is depicted as a simple-
minded son of the priesthood who was driven to despera-
tion by the burning of his house and chapel by yeomen
cavalry. His followers believed he was possessed of super-
natural powers, that he could catch bullets with his fingers.
   He rapidly took Oulart, Camolin, and Ferns with a half-
starved rebel army armed mainly with pikes. Following
these successes he captured Enniscorthy after a big battle
and camped on Vinegar Hill above the town. On May 30,
driving all before him, he took Wexford itself. But the
loyalists who supported the British Crown began to or-
ganize, and British troops were shipped into Ireland in vast
numbers. After further successes came defeat. Father John,
with hundreds of others, many of them priests, was exe-
cuted. His death broke the myth of his believed invinci-
bility.

THEOBALD WOLFE TONE   One of the greatest names of Irish
history, Theobald Wolfe Tone, a United Irishman, was in

France serving under Napoleon in the French army when the 1798 rebellion broke out under Lord Edward Fitzgerald. Earlier, in 1796, Tone managed to persuade the French Directory in Paris to send an invasion fleet to Ireland to support a previous rebellion. On December 15, 1796, this fleet set sail from Brest with 15,000 men, seventeen large warships, and thirteen frigates. Had this great fleet landed in Ireland, it undoubtedly would have changed the course of Irish history, for the peasants were seething under the cruelty of English rule. However, tempestuous weather was encountered and, broken and battered, the invaders struggled back to Brest.

This was a serious setback in Wolfe Tone's plans. But in August 1798, as a result of his further endeavours, Napoleon sent another invasion force to Ireland under General Humbert. It was a small force but it managed to land immediately and defeated a British force twice its size. But the rebellion under Lord Edward Fitzgerald was now broken and ended, Ireland was full of British troops, and the French general soon had to surrender. Wolfe Tone persuaded yet another force of Frenchmen to attempt an invasion of Ireland two months later, and sailed with this fleet himself. But the French were attacked by a British squadron and were defeated. Tone was taken prisoner, conveyed to Dublin, and there tried and sentenced to be hanged. He asked for a soldier's death by shooting: this was refused and in October 1798, he committed suicide with a tiny knife he had managed to obtain.

Mention is made of O'Connor, Emmet, Sweetman, Neilson, Michael Reynolds, and Lawless. These were all United Irishmen prominent in the fight for Irish independence.

Mention is made of yeomanry and militia. These were mainly Irish by nationality; local regiments composed of farmers and the sons and employees of landowners who supported the British Crown and who assisted troops in opposing the demands of the United Irishmen and in putting down the peasantry. Of these Irish forces the North Cork Militia under Lord Kingsborough was the most hated and feared, and their treatment of the peasants was largely responsible for the viciousness of the rebel revenge.

The French Revolution and the 1798 Irish rebellion had common aims. Whereas the former was a revolution against the cruelty and oppression of the aristocracy, the latter was an attempt by Ireland to throw off the yoke and tyranny of British rule which was supporting a system which enriched the landlords and impoverished the peasants.

DATE DUE

GAYLORD   PRINTED IN U.S.A.